THE
REPLACEMENT

Also by Lindsey Duga

The Haunting

Ghost in the Headlights

THE
REPLACEMENT

LINDSEY DUGA

Scholastic Inc.

ISBN 978-1-338-84666-9

10 9 8 7 6 5 4 3 2 1   22 23 24 25 26

Printed in the U.S.A.   40
First printing 2022

Book design by Stephanie Yang

To Aunt Mae

Prologue

The flashlight was out of batteries. It was an old thing, so one set never lasted very long, but it felt like Paula had just put some new ones in the other day. Annoyed, she slapped the cool metal head against her palm. The light flickered, illuminating the world under the covers for but a moment before it all went dark again.

"Useless thing," Paula hissed into her pillow as she attempted to shake it. Unfortunately, the light stayed out. Maybe for good this time.

Outside, the autumn wind blew, harsh and unforgiving through the bare branches of the trees. The creepy tapping sound, like someone was rapping on the window, wanting in, echoed through the room and all the way under her covers.

No one's there, Paula reminded herself, hugging her stuffed teddy bear tightly to her chest. *It's the branches against the glass. That's all.*

"Paula?" came a voice from the darkness.

The covers were yanked back, exposing Paula to the chilly night air of the house. If it hadn't been for the familiar tone of her sister's voice, Paula would've screamed. The black silhouette, framed against the faint moonlight coming from the window, would've been frightful to anyone, but Paula was a scaredy-cat by nature.

"What are you still doing up?" her sister, Patty, asked, reaching over to turn on the bedside lamp.

Golden light filled the bedroom and the shadows ran back into the corners, stretching up their long dark fingers into the rafters. Paula tried to ignore the shadows, but she kept an eye on them. Just in case.

"I was just gonna read a little," Paula said as Patty sat on the edge of the bed.

"Liar." Patty took the flashlight from her sister and dug into the pocket of her yellow rose-print pajamas. She pulled out a pair of batteries and popped the bottom off the flashlight. Like she'd done it a thousand times, Patty slid out the old batteries and inserted new ones. The flashlight bulb brightened, shining a wide circle of white light on the ceiling.

"You got scared, didn't you? Was it the wind?" Patty asked as she handed the flashlight back to Paula.

With a frown, Paula accepted the flashlight and shrugged. "It wouldn't be so bad if Papa would cut down the tree branches."

As if on cue, the wind howled and the branches went wild. Now it sounded like there wasn't just one person tapping on the glass, but five. All clacking, and rapping, and tapping—desperate to get inside.

Paula shrank back, pulling the covers up to her nose, while Patty shook her head, her blonde curls swishing. "I wish Mama and Papa wouldn't have given us different bedrooms," Patty said. "You slept better when we were together."

"We're old enough now to have separate bedrooms," Paula said, not wanting to admit the real reason they were separated. It would make her cry, and she didn't want to cry tonight.

Patty grinned and tapped the head of the stuffed bear in Paula's arms. "But young enough to sleep with stuffed animals?"

Paula smiled back and held out her teddy bear, lifting his arm in a mock salute. To give her toy a voice, she dropped hers to a low gruff tone. "I protect Princess Paula from the monsters outside, Princess Patty."

Patty opened her mouth to reply, but just then another gust of wind tore through their backyard and the branches raked across the glass, scratching horridly. Paula whimpered and tugged the covers up over her head.

But her sister only pulled them back down again. "That's it. Get up. Come to the window—I want to show you something."

"Absolutely not."

"C'mon, P. I swear it's not scary. It's a surprise."

Paula peeked out from under the covers. "Promise?"

Her twin sister smiled. "Promise, with a capital P."

Reluctantly, Paula swung her legs over the side of the bed and padded across the woven rug to where her sister stood by the window. She left her bear on the bed. She didn't need his protection when her sister was with her. Patty would protect Paula from anything.

At the window, they looked out into their dark backyard. A

lawn covered with red, yellow, orange, and brown autumn leaves extended out before them with a great big oak tree standing in the center. A cloud passed above, revealing the half-moon in a blanket of inky blackness. The leaves stirred with another bout of wind and the branches hit the window, right next to Paula's face. She flinched back, but Patty kept hold of her hand, squeezing it tight.

With her free hand, Patty pointed out at the big tree. "Papa promised to build us a treehouse in the spring. Right in our tree."

Paula gasped with delight. "Really? When did he tell you?"

"Today. After the doctor's. He promised. And you know what that means."

The two sisters grinned at each other and recited together: "Everyone in Pemblebrook keeps their promises."

They burst into a fit of giggles, but just as quickly, Patty's laughter turned into coughs. Big, hacking, wet coughs that shook her lungs and made her sway on her feet and drop to her knees. Immediately, Paula knelt next to her sister, rubbing her back, but not knowing what to do. When the coughs took hold, nothing seemed to stop them.

Just a few seconds later, their parents rushed through the door, crowding Patty while Paula stepped back to let them.

She watched, helpless, as her father picked up Patty and took her back to her room. The room that had been given to Patty ever since she got sick. Ever since the doctors started giving her bad-tasting medicine, and refusing to let her play outside. It had been months. And none of it was working.

Paula listened in the hallway as her parents gave Patty her medicine and tucked her back into bed. It was a while later before the coughing finally stopped and Paula was able to slip into her sister's room without her parents noticing.

Patty smiled at Paula's entrance and slid over in the bed. It was their ritual. They slept in the same bed almost every night. Though neither of them said it, they both knew why. They wanted to spend whatever time they had left together.

Huddled in bed, they pulled the covers over their heads as Paula turned on the flashlight.

"You're going to get better . . . right, Pat?"

Patty smiled, gripping her sister's hand and squeezing it. "I have to, P. We're going to play in that treehouse all summer."

Paula squeezed right back. "It's a prom—"

But her last word was drowned out by another moan of wind. It sounded like an old witch, howling in pain, and as a stray branch hit the window so hard it made the wooden frame rattle, Paula ducked her head under the covers. Patty didn't even flinch next to her. She was always the braver one.

1

Seventy years later . . .

Erin stepped out of the car onto the gravel driveway of·their new home. It had seemed like only yesterday when her mother told her about the move.

She had been looking for her favorite striped sweater, annoyed as she tossed another stuffed animal to the side. This one was a giraffe. His name was Mr. Fuzzy Hooves and he was the bane of Erin's existence. Him, Mrs. Snow Whiskers, Mr. Purple Tooth, Lady Daisy, and Ned. They were always mixed among Erin's things like little animal invaders.

But that's what happened when you shared a room with your five-year-old sister: There were no sides. There were just Becca's toys, and they were always everywhere.

"Mom!" Erin had hollered. "I can't find my striped sweater!"

There was no answer. Her mother didn't believe in yelling, at least, not unless it was for emergencies. So, with yet another groan, Erin stomped from her bedroom, down the narrow hall of their small apartment to the living room, where her mother sat on the couch, folding laundry.

"Mom, I can't find my striped sweater," Erin repeated.

Her mother didn't even look up from folding a pair of pants. "It's in the wash."

"But why? It wasn't even dirty!"

"Becca spilled cranberry juice on it."

Erin fought back the urge to yell. Her mother would only scold her and say the same thing she said every time Becca ruined one of Erin's things: "Remember, all things can be replaced."

Erin always hated hearing that. Probably because it was rare that her parents actually replaced anything of Erin's that Becca ruined.

"But I wanted to wear it to the park with Sarah this afternoon."

Her mother gave her a sympathetic look, but that didn't

magically make the sweater clean again. "Sorry, honey. Wear your purple sweater."

"Never mind," Erin grumbled, as she started to turn back down the hall. "I'll just hang out in my room."

"Erin? Come back, I want to tell you something."

Immediately, Erin sensed the tone change in her mother's voice. It was her "serious" voice, and it usually came with bad news. Like when Erin had to get her tonsils taken out, or when she couldn't go to a Chicago Cubs game with her friend Sarah because her parents needed her to stay home and watch Becca while they went to her father's company dinner.

With a feeling of dread, Erin came back into the living room. Her mother patted the spot on the couch beside her and Erin sat.

"Yeah?" Erin asked, not wanting to know what her mother had to say.

"We were going to tell the both of you at dinner, but I realized that it's not always fair that we treat you and Becca the same. You're older than her, of course, so you might react differently to things, and we should devote just as much attention to your feelings—"

"Mom," Erin interrupted, feeling more anxious by the second. "Just tell me."

"Your father got a new job."

Erin blinked. That was usually good news, right? So why was her mother using her "serious" voice?

"His position will be much different than before. He'll be able to work from home. That means he'll need an office."

Erin wasn't entirely sure where this was going. Her mother already had an office—and she needed one for her work. Laura Dodgeson was an accomplished therapist and wrote an ongoing book series on child therapy.

"What I'm trying to say, honey, is that we no longer need to live in the city. We found a house outside Chicago that is just lovely. It's in a town called Pemblebrook. I know it will be a change, but it will be a good one. You can have your own room, and . . ."

Erin hardly heard anything after that. Though moving might've been bad news to most twelve-year-olds, Erin was actually *thrilled*. Sure, it was going to be sad leaving Sarah, but Erin didn't have many other friends—partly because she had to take care of Becca so much that she missed hanging out with her classmates after school. And it wasn't exactly that she *hated*

Chicago, but ever since last summer when they'd visited Aunt Katharine in the countryside of Illinois, Erin couldn't wait to go back.

Every day there had been something different to do. She'd watched the minnows swim over the shiny pebbles in the creek behind her aunt's house. They'd flown kites over small hills covered in clovers and taken long nature paths through the woods.

It had been so free and fun outside the confinement of the city's concrete borders.

Living out in a small town, in their own house, with their own backyard, and—most importantly—her own room, was basically a dream come true.

And now, standing there in front of the house, Erin had to admit that the photos from the real estate agent's website hadn't done it justice. It seemed taller than the pictures, reaching up to almost brush the blue June sky. Small sparrows flitted across the roof, and then perched on the rain gutters, chirping a chorus of broken songs. It was a two-story house, and had pale blue-gray siding, a white wraparound porch, and a redbrick chimney. In the early afternoon, the sunlight glinted off the windows and cast shadows from the few trees that surrounded their property. They were the last house at the end of a long lane with loads of space between each home.

While driving out of Chicago on their way to Pemblebrook, Erin hadn't once looked back at the towering skyscrapers made of steel and glass. She was too busy looking toward the rolling green hills of summertime Illinois. So naturally she hadn't slept a wink throughout the car trip, even though it had been over three hours long.

The Dodgesons had drank in the sights of their new town. Pemblebrook seemed to have everything: Sprawling parks with soccer fields and tennis courts, charming streets with local shops and restaurants, a public library, a movie theater, a skating rink—it was the perfect place. Halfway through the town, her parents pointed out what would be Erin's new school in the fall, and Erin actually found herself excited—even about something as boring as school.

"Erin! Erin! Look! Look!" Becca cried, pulling Erin's attention away from the house to the backyard—literally. Her little sister yanked on Erin's arm so hard it bordered on painful, not to mention annoying.

It wasn't hard to see what had Becca all riled up. In the center of their very large backyard was a very large oak tree. It had big sprawling branches that dipped low to the earth, almost like they were knobby elbows looking for a rest. The trunk stretched up ten, maybe twelve feet, before it divided off into the large, thick branches. And while the big oak tree was beautiful in of itself, it was not the most exciting thing in the backyard.

Wedged in the center of the oak tree, between two massive branches, was a little house made of sanded yellowwood planks. It was about the size for a child Erin's age, complete with a window and checkered curtains. More wooden planks had been nailed into the trunk as a makeshift ladder that traveled up to what Erin assumed had to be the door into the treehouse.

"Wow," Erin breathed.

"Yeah, wow," Becca repeated.

The two girls raced across the backyard to the tree, their footsteps flattening the soft green grass.

"Me first! Me first!" Becca grabbed hold of the first wooden plank and started her journey up. Erin wasn't going to argue; she knew she needed to stay below her sister in case Becca accidentally slipped and fell.

But, about four planks up, Becca froze.

"Erin?" she said in a small voice. "I changed my mind. Can I get back down?"

"Sure," Erin said, confused. "Just step back down, I've got you."

As Becca started her descent, Erin placed a hand on her back for safety. Strangely, her sister's back wasn't warm through her clothes. It was chilly. Like touching a cold stone.

Once she'd returned to solid ground, Becca folded her arms. She was uncommonly quiet.

"Becks? What's wrong?" Erin asked.

Before Becca could answer, their mother's voice carried across the lawn. "Erin? Becca? Don't you want to see inside?"

"Coming!" Becca shouted as she turned right around and sprinted toward the house.

Erin hesitated. Becca's retreat from the treehouse had certainly been strange—Erin had never known her younger sister to back down from anything. Even high jungle gyms on the playground. And though she badly wanted to go up into the treehouse, she more desperately wanted to see her new room. So, with only a small ounce of reluctance, she hurried to the back door, where her mother stood waiting.

Erin's new room was everything she'd hoped. It was big, with enough room for her twin bed, a desk, her own dresser, and a nightstand. She even had a closet. Becca's room was about the same size and right across from their parents. The kitchen, bathrooms, and carpets all looked brand-new, while the walls simply needed a fresh coat of paint and the wooden floors looked worn but durable—which their mother thought added to the house's charm.

After a packed lunch of sandwiches, Erin and Becca sat on the back part of the porch with Becca's animals spread around them in tea party formation. Their parents had asked Erin to play with Becca while they instructed the movers. While Erin understood why it wasn't a good idea for them to be around while the movers came in and out of the house rolling dollies and carrying boxes, it didn't stop her from feeling a little bitter. She wanted to be unpacking her room and hanging up her posters and *National Geographic* photo collage. It was so exciting to have a space of her own, and now that it was right within her reach, she still had to wait.

"Lady Daisy," Becca said in her prim and proper voice, as she spoke to the stuffed yellow elephant. "Would you like some sugar in your tea?"

"Oh," Erin said, only just then remembering that she was supposed to be playing as Lady Daisy. Erin lowered her voice an octave and moved the elephant's head in a firm nod. "Why, thank you, Miss Becca."

Becca rose up on her knees to lean over and pretend to dish out a spoonful of sugar from her plastic sugar pot into Lady Daisy's plastic tea cup. But then she stopped, her gaze locked on a spot over Erin's head.

Erin looked behind her. "Becca? What is it?"

At her name, Becca flinched, knocking over her glass of lemonade left from lunch.

"Let me get some paper towels. I'll be right back." Rolling her eyes, Erin hopped to her feet and dashed into the kitchen. She was used to cleaning up Becca's spills. By the time she returned though, Becca was not on the porch.

For a brief moment, Erin panicked, but then she spotted her—out in the middle of the backyard in front of the oak tree. Just . . . standing there.

Becca wasn't a stand-still sort of kid. She was here, there, and everywhere, so it was strange that she was frozen like that. Dropping the paper towels on the spilled lemonade, Erin made her way down the porch steps and across the grass to where Becca stood, unmoving.

Even when Erin got close, Becca didn't turn to look at her, or acknowledge her presence in any way. The look on Becca's face—vacant and dead—gave Erin chills. She'd never seen her sister like this before. Becca's eyes were fixated on a spot above, and her lips were parted slightly, like she was halfway through a gasp.

Erin turned to look in the direction that Becca was staring at, but saw nothing strange about the tree or the treehouse. It was just as it had been before, empty and full of golden sunlight.

"Becca?" Erin bent down to be level with the little girl. "Are you okay? Talk to me."

In response, Becca raised one arm and pointed into the tree, right at the treehouse window.

"What are you—" Erin turned to look again, but stopped as her pulse stuttered.

There was someone in the window.

2

There hadn't been anyone in the window just a few seconds before, Erin was sure of it. She would've noticed. Squinting, Erin placed a hand over her eyes to shield the sunlight, thinking that maybe it was a trick of the tree's shadows. But the silhouette didn't go away. If anything, it sharpened into the profile of a young girl. She couldn't quite make out the girl's features due to the shadowy interior of the treehouse, but she could see a hand pushing aside the checkered curtains and the outline of gold curls.

Who was this girl and why was she in their treehouse? *Maybe she's a neighbor,* Erin thought.

"Hey!" Erin shouted up at the girl. "We just moved here. Do you live next door?"

The girl just dropped her hand, letting the checkered

curtains fall into place. But her shadow remained behind the curtain, so Erin assumed maybe she was coming down to talk.

Except no one came down.

Now Erin was starting to get a little annoyed. At this point, the girl was being plain rude. She was ignoring Erin, maybe even thinking that Erin was going to give up and go away.

Well, that definitely wasn't going to happen. This was *their* treehouse now, after all.

Erin turned to Becca. "You stay down here, okay?"

Again, Becca didn't move, or even nod. She still wore that strange vacant look.

With a frown, Erin stalked toward the tree and grabbed the first plank and hoisted herself up. A stirring of wind ruffled the grass below her feet, the leaves above her head and the ends of the her hair on her shoulders. It was a chilly breeze for a summer day, giving Erin goose bumps on her neck and arms. Still, she continued upward into the tree, gripping each plank one by one to reach the bottom of the treehouse.

Sure enough, there was an opening cut out in the wood floor directly above her. Erin poked her head through. "Hello?"

At once, a chill rippled down her spine. It was sharp and

sudden and made all the goose bumps she had multiply. The hair on her arms and the back of her neck stood straight up, prickling her skin and tightening it, almost painfully.

But the strange chill was not Erin's main concern. Now that she could see fully into the treehouse, it was very apparent that no one was inside.

How was that possible? Erin had *seen* the girl in the window. Watched her drop the curtain. Noticed the curve of her profile and the golden hue of her curls in the sunlight.

Yet somehow, the treehouse seemed totally empty.

With one heave, Erin pulled herself up through the door and into the treehouse. It was tall enough for her to stand comfortably, and wide enough to fit a bookshelf. The corners were shadowy and full of cobwebs, and the wood floor was covered in a thick layer of dust. As far as Erin could tell, no one had been up here in many, many years.

It was also extremely cold. Frigid, even. Erin couldn't actually believe how icy the air felt. Sure, it was shadowy, thanks to all the leaves in the oak tree, but it felt like the interior of a freezer or a day in December. Definitely not in June.

Shivering, Erin took a few steps over to the window and

yanked the curtain back. She could see Becca was in the same place she'd left her. From this height, their new house seemed even larger, and the driveway out to the road looked long and lonely.

"Erin!"

Becca's shout didn't have the usual excitement in it. It sounded more frantic, even a bit . . . fearful.

"I'm right here," Erin said with a wave and a smile in an attempt to reassure her little sister. She couldn't figure out what had Becca acting so strange. Maybe she was jealous that Erin was up here, and *she* wasn't, not having gone up herself. But that didn't explain the fear.

"Erin!" Becca cried again, even more panicked and urgent this time.

"Okay, okay, I'm coming," Erin called back, taking one more look at their new house and backyard. But just as she was about to turn away from the window, Erin felt something that froze her where she stood:

Someone's fingers running through her hair.

With a gasp, Erin whirled around, her hand flying to her hair, pressing the back of her neck.

No one was there. Just like before, the treehouse was vacant and still.

Erin's heart pounded unsteadily, as she kept her hand flat against her short brown hair. Had that been the wind? No... Erin knew the sensation well. When she was younger, her mother used to run her fingers through her hair all the time as a way to help Erin go to sleep after a bad dream. And that had definitely been someone's fingers threading through her locks. Even the touch of fingertips on the back of her neck had felt so real.

But how could Erin argue with her own eyes? No one was in the treehouse, therefore no one could've touched her.

With a hard swallow, Erin hurried to lower herself through the door and climbed quickly down the wooden planks. As soon as her feet touched the ground, Becca was at her side, grabbing her hand and yanking her toward the house. This time, Erin didn't mind at all.

Erin didn't think about the treehouse for a whole week. Sure, the thought of it tickled the back of her mind occasionally when she was out in the backyard with Becca, but for the most part, she was too busy helping around their new house. It was a welcome distraction.

Their mother, Mrs. Dodgeson, had been in a cleaning frenzy. The house, while not exactly filthy, did need a lot of work when you looked closer. Mold was in the cracks of the bathroom tiles, and grime coated the stove and oven. Dust was in the dining and living room rafters and the closets smelled of mothballs. Erin helped where she could—like cleaning the windows and mirrors so they were smudge-free—but her main job was watching Becca and making sure the five-year-old didn't get into things like buckets of paint.

Her parents had chosen a soft cream color for the walls, which really brightened the place up. The sunlight that streamed through the windows touched the vanilla hue, and it made the rooms glow with warmth. With new paint, it looked like a brand-new house.

After the repainting and cleaning came unpacking. Erin took great effort in her room. She spent hours studying her walls and making sure every photo of her *National Geographic* collage was in the right spot. She wanted to tell a story across the globe, from Antelope Canyon in Arizona, to Angel Falls in

Venezuela, to the Frozen Sea in Sweden. She alphabetized her bookshelf and made sure her clothes were folded and hung neatly in her dresser and closet. Every time she unpacked an item and placed it in its new spot, she took great satisfaction knowing that it would stay there. Her little sister had her own room now with her own space to mess things up, instead of Erin's.

Almost every day, a new piece of furniture was delivered to the house. Most shipments were for her father's new office, but now that they lived in a spacious house, they could fill it with things like a coffee table, or end table, or the armchair her father always wanted. Her mother was also constantly ordering things online to help with the decoration and upkeep of their new home. Because of that, Erin was the one tasked to check the mailbox at the end of their long driveway.

It was one morning while checking the mail that Erin met the first kid on their street—a Black girl around Erin's own age who was practicing tricks on her skateboard. Erin had never skateboarded, but she'd always wanted to try, so she found herself staring. The girl noticed her too and gave her a wave. Erin waved back, wondering if she should walk over and introduce herself. Luckily, she didn't have to decide, because the girl skateboarded right over to the mailbox where Erin was standing.

Now that she was closer, Erin took in the girl's appearance. She wore her hair in braids underneath her helmet and had on a blue soccer jersey. Immediately, Erin wished she would've changed out of her faded sleepshirt with an old video game logo on it.

The girl's lips hitched up in a smile. "Cool shirt."

Erin smiled back, since the compliment sounded sincere. "Thanks."

She stepped off her skateboard and flipped it up with the toe of her sneaker. "I'm Tara. You just moved in?"

"Yeah, I'm Erin. Nice to meet you."

"You too," Tara replied, but her gaze wasn't on Erin, it was far behind her. Like she was staring at her house, or even farther back.

Erin was reminded of Becca's look at the treehouse—how it had been focused on something . . . not quite there.

"Gotta say," Tara said, tearing her gaze away from wherever she'd been staring to focus on Erin, "never thought anyone would actually move in here."

Erin frowned, instantly feeling annoyed. Was this girl some-how insulting her new house? Erin may have only been living in it for a few days, but she was already in love with it.

"Why's that?" she asked, trying not to sound snippy.

"You moved from out of town, right?" Tara asked, completely ignoring Erin's question.

"Yeah, Chicago," Erin said.

"That explains it."

Explains what? Erin wanted to retort, but she didn't want her question ignored again. More than that, she didn't want to hear anything bad this girl had to say about her house. Maybe she was being a little overly sensitive, but now that this house was *hers*, anything said against it felt personal.

Thinking of a way to change the subject, Erin remembered the mysterious girl in the treehouse. "So..." she began, trying to figure out how best to ask what she had on her mind. "Do any other kids live around here?"

Tara nodded. "Samuel and Zach, but they're older. High school."

That was definitely strange. If Tara was the only other girl around here, then who did Erin see in the treehouse?

As if reading her thoughts, Tara asked suddenly, "You went in the treehouse, didn't you?"

Erin blinked, surprised. "Yeah . . ."

Tara shifted from foot to foot. Finally, she leaned closer and said in a low voice, "I would . . . stay out of it. Like, *seriously*."

Again, irritation prickled Erin's nerves. *Is she trying to scare me?* Erin wondered. Did this warning have something to do with her comment about people never moving in? If it did, Erin didn't want to hear any more. She wasn't going to let anyone ruin her new home.

"Sure." Erin clutched the stack of mail tighter to her chest. "Well, my breakfast is getting cold. I'll see you around."

Tara frowned. It was an obvious excuse, but Tara didn't stop Erin as she turned and walked back down her long driveway to her house.

Erin decided then and there to just forget about this whole interaction, and the next time she saw Tara, they could start over. But in the back of her mind, Tara's warning reminded Erin of the sensation she had felt in the treehouse—of someone grazing their cold fingertips on the back of her neck.

Unconsciously, she shivered.

3

The Monday following their big move, Erin's mother and father were ready to go back to work. It was a little odd though, considering Erin was so used to her father waking up early and jetting off to catch the seven thirty a.m. train. Instead, he woke up later, put on a nice button-down with sweatpants, and had a leisurely breakfast of French toast with them. Then he announced he was off to work and simply walked right down the hall into his new office.

"So, what do you girls plan to do today?" Mrs. Dodgeson asked as she began running water in the sink to wash that morning's breakfast dishes.

Erin stacked their plates from the table and brought them to the sink while Becca hunched over her coloring book and scribbled with a blue crayon onto a princess's dress. "I was thinking of exploring the neighborhood," Erin said. Maybe she'd run into Tara again, and maybe Erin could try out her skateboard this time.

Her mother hummed for a moment and Erin knew that was a bad sign. Mrs. Dodgeson did that when she was thinking of a nice way of saying no.

"Why don't you wait until your father and I can go with you? It will be a nice family walk."

Erin bit her lip to stop the almost-immediate whine that threatened to seep out her mouth. She wanted to go by herself. Her mother was *always* finding ways of turning things into a "family event" when Erin was perfectly happy exploring or spending time independently. This mostly had to do with the fact that anytime it was a family outing, Becca soaked up most of the attention anyway, as five-year-olds did.

"Besides," her mother continued, "it rained most of last night and you don't want to get your sneakers muddy."

Erin wanted to point out that they lived in the country now. Muddy sneakers and grass stains were going to be a way of life. But her mother liked things to be clean, so Erin thought it best not to mention it.

"Okaaaay," Erin said slowly, drawing out the word. What else could she do? Something preferably without Becca. She was determined not to let her mother ruin her first real day of exploration.

That was when the treehouse jumped back into her mind.

"How about the treehouse? Can I read up there for a while?"

Unfortunately, Tara's warning popped up in her mind as well, but Erin quickly shoved it away. Whatever rumor there was about her house or the treehouse wasn't worth believing in, or even hearing. At her old school in Chicago, there was a rumor that the second-floor girls' bathroom was haunted. It just turned out to be a loose hinge on a stall door, so it opened with a loud creak even when no one was there.

And whatever happened that day in the treehouse had probably just been a trick with the shadows and wind. There were all kinds of country sights and sounds she wasn't used to yet.

Her mother brightened as she scrubbed the dirty pan with a soapy washcloth. "That sounds lovely. You and Becca can—"

"I'm going to work on a puzzle in my room," Becca announced. Then she stood with her coloring book and set of crayons and hurried from the kitchen.

Erin and Mrs. Dodgeson both watched the doorway, where Becca had just disappeared. They could hear her loud footsteps stomping up the stairs.

What's with her? Erin thought.

It was a little odd. Erin couldn't remember the last time that Becca chose to do something by herself. Becca was always bugging Erin to do things together. Play dolls, watch TV, read, color, play board games, even take baths—always together. Sometimes it drove Erin crazy, so hearing her little sister reject Erin's plans was a little like music to her ears.

Erin looked back to her mother, eyes wide with hope.

"Wellll," Mrs. Dodgeson said slowly, drawing out the word, and sounding just like her daughter. "Then I suppose you can spend a few hours in the treehouse. Luckily I don't have any meetings this morning, so I can listen for Becca if she needs anything."

It took all the restraint Erin had to not jump and shout with triumph. *Yes! I'm little-sister-free!* Erin shouted in her head, then amended, *at least for a few hours.*

"Before you go out, I need you to label and tape up the boxes in the hallway for Goodwill. Dad found some old items in the attic that we can get rid of. I contacted the real estate agent to see if we needed to mail them to the previous family, but she said not to bother. Wonder why." With a click of her tongue, Mrs. Dodgeson opened a kitchen drawer and pulled out a large black marker and a roll of packing tape and handed them both to Erin. "Here you go, honey. Once you finish this, you can go to the treehouse."

With a ruffle of Erin's hair, Mrs. Dodgeson headed up the stairs as well, her steps much lighter and more graceful than Becca's.

When packing up their own house, Erin had plenty of practice in labeling boxes. Her mother praised her nice, clear handwriting, so Erin didn't really mind. Besides, large perma-nent markers were fun to write with.

She started with the box closest to the stairs. Its con-tents were some old board games, and office supplies like a clunky flashlight that looked like it was over fifty years old, along with a set of rulers, and a stack of old spiral-bound notebooks with scribbles. She also found a teddy bear that looked old and dusty, but well cared-for. Clearly loved. Erin considered setting it aside for Becca, because out of all the stuffed animals her little sister had, she didn't have a bear.

"She's got enough stuffed animals already," Erin muttered to herself. So she put the bear back in the box.

The most interesting thing by far was an old globe that spun around with a slight rusty squeak. That one, she saved. She couldn't let such a cool, old find get tossed out. She'd clean it and ask her dad to stop the squeaking and it would be as good as new.

Setting aside the old globe, she taped up the box and labeled it as GAMES AND OFFICE SUPPLIES. She went through the three other boxes, each one getting their own label—KITCHENWARE, CLOTHES, and BEDDING.

Once Erin was done with her task, she put the marker and the packing tape on top of the boxes, then grabbed the globe and hurried upstairs to her room and set it on her desk.

"I'll find a place for you later," she told the old globe, then she grabbed her backpack and started stuffing it with various things she wanted to leave up in the treehouse. On her way outside, Erin paused to put on her sneakers. Because Mrs. Dodgeson loved having spotless floors, she made sure all her family took their shoes off at the door so they wouldn't track dirt or mud through the house.

Erin headed out the door and jogged across the backyard. Immediately, she could tell her mother had been right: It *had* rained a lot last night. Even with a few steps through the soft grass, dew drenched her ankle socks and she could feel her sneakers sink into the wet mud. The scent of rain was also thick in the air, and at one point, her footsteps made a suction noise as she stepped in a particularly muddy spot. She'd definitely have to clean her shoes before going back in the house. Birds chirped loudly above her, and as she grabbed the first plank and hoisted herself up, Erin wondered just how many of them made their home in this massive tree.

The climb up was as easy as the first time she'd done it, but once again, she felt the beginnings of a chill despite the morning sunrise to warm her back. As she reached the door of the treehouse and poked her head through, all bird chirping went deadly silent. How the birds stopped all at once and all together, Erin had no idea. All she *did* know was that it was eerie. It was like the noise from the outside world just stopped, like a sound-proof door slamming shut.

Maybe there was a stray cat that had scared them into silence or something.

With a shrug, Erin boosted herself up into the treehouse. It was just how she left it last time. Empty, shadowy paint-peeling walls, with the checkered curtains in place, and dust coating the wood floor. Even the footsteps she'd made the last time she'd come were already fading into another layer of dust. Whoever she'd seen in the window hadn't been there recently, or hadn't been there at all.

Erin dropped her backpack on the floor with a thud and crossed to the window, rubbing her arms. "Geez, why's it so cold?" she grumbled. It was just as cold as last time. But she chalked up the icy temperature to the night before and the rain. What else could it be? It wasn't as if the treehouse had an air conditioner or a freezer.

She pushed the curtains to the side, letting in the sunlight. The shadows were vanquished and Erin could feel a hint of warmth touch her chilly skin. Satisfied, she turned to her backpack and started to pull out her things. After dusting off the area with a brush of her palm, she set a stack of books and *National Geographic* magazines off in a corner. She set the binoculars that Aunt Katharine had gifted to her last Christmas on the window ledge so she could reach them easily for bird-watching or neighbor-spying. The last thing she pulled out was her Amazon rainforest poster and her packet of thumbtacks.

As she surveyed the walls of the treehouse for a place to hang her poster, something caught her eye on the left wall.

It was faded, but the tale-tell signs of scratched words could be seen through the old white peeling paint. Erin stepped closer to take a look and squinted at the misshaped letters.

PATTY + P———

The first word was clearly a person's name. Patty. Immediately, Erin's thoughts went to the girl that Erin had thought she'd seen in the treehouse last week. Could that be her? But what about the second name? Or at least, she assumed it was a name. Maybe not. The only thing she could tell was the first letter—*P*. The rest of the word was so scratched out that it was impossible to read. In fact, it seemed as though someone had scratched out the rest of the name with a lot of anger. More than a hundred strokes into the wood were carved through the letters. As if to erase the existence of that person entirely . . .

"Weird," Erin said under her breath. Just another thing to

add to the ever-growing list of oddities about this treehouse.

Deciding she didn't want to look at the weird scratches of a previous owner, Erin held up the Amazon poster and pressed thumbtacks into the corners, covering it up. With a smile, Erin stepped back to admire it. Without much effort, the poster was only slightly crooked. Barely noticeable, really. And the lush green rainforest brought color to the dull interior of the treehouse.

Erin sat down and reached for one of her books. She could read here, uninterrupted, all morning. But she hadn't even made it to the second page before a wave of sleepiness hit her.

She'd been awake for only a couple hours, but somehow she was already exhausted. Yawning, Erin set the book down and lay on her side. She shivered and curled inward—the intense cold was back, but she was too tired to get up and leave for her own warm bed for a nap.

As her eyelids fluttered closed, a dark shadow emerged from the corner of the treehouse. She blinked heavily and the shadow became more pronounced. The form of a person, bending over her.

Erin's heart pounded inside her chest. She wanted to scream, or maybe get up and run from the sudden figure who had emerged from the shadows like it was part of them—but she couldn't move, almost as if her body was locked up tight. She could only see and hear—hear the soft, raspy breathing of the shadowy figure and the creak of the wood as it knelt down and reached out an opaque hand toward Erin.

As the hand drew closer, Erin couldn't keep her eyes open any longer, even as panicked as she was. The moment she closed them, sleep took hold.

4

The sound of birds chirping woke Erin. With a soft groan, she lifted her head and looked around, trying to remember where she was. Her sleep had come on so fast, and so hard, it left her feeling disoriented. Her vision was hazy, merely shapes of colors and shades.

That was when she remembered—the person! The figure made of shadows, bending over her and reaching for her like it was going to touch her. Was it still around?

"Um ... Hello?" she asked, her voice trembling a little as she sat up and squinted through her bleary vision. Slowly, the blurred edges began to sharpen.

She was in the treehouse, that was for sure, but ... it didn't feel quite the same. The silence was gone. Birds chirped outside and the buzzing of insects sounded deafening in her ears. The chill was also gone. It was warm, even hot, and stuffy. She'd definitely remembered being freezing cold before she'd fallen asleep. Had it warmed up that quickly? Just how long had she been asleep? Sunlight still streamed through the open window, which meant it couldn't be that late in the afternoon. Not to mention, there's no way her mother would've let her stay up here past lunchtime.

When she was certain she was alone in the treehouse, Erin got to her feet, feeling stiff—probably from sleeping on the hard wood. She went to brush off the dust along her shorts, but there was none. That was the other thing that felt different about the treehouse: It looked brand-new. Where the paint had been faded and peeling, it was now smooth and clean. It even smelled like a fresh coat of paint, and she should know— they'd been painting the new house for almost an entire week. The checkered curtains weren't moth-eaten or dingy either. They were ironed and vibrant, as if someone had just sewn them and hung them.

What was more, all her things were gone. Her rainforest poster, her stack of books and binoculars...everything was missing.

"What's going on?" Erin muttered to herself. She was more than a little confused, but she didn't know what else to do other than to go back into the house and find her parents. At the very least, she should tell them that someone had stolen her things.

Still feeling slightly foggy from her nap, Erin slipped through the opening in the treehouse door and climbed down the trunk using the wooden planks—which also felt freshly sanded. The moment her foot touched the grass, a shout sent her heart racing.

"There you are!"

Erin whirled around, about to scold Becca for surprising her, but her sister's name died on her lips.

It wasn't Becca, or her parents, but a total stranger.

A girl, maybe a year or two younger than Erin, stood just a few feet away. Her skin was white with rosy pink cheeks, while her hair was long and blonde and curly, tied back in a pink ribbon. She wore a rather frilly dress. Her white socks were ruffled and she wore shiny black shoes with buckles. Immediately, Erin thought the clothes looked old-fashioned. She didn't know any girls around her age who would ever wear that frilly of a dress.

"Um, hi," Erin said to the girl. "Are you my neighbor?"

The girl placed her hands on her hips and tilted her head, giving Erin a strange look. "What are you talking about? How could you have forgotten who I am?"

Erin's confusion doubled. She was fairly sure she'd never met this girl. But her mind was so foggy in that moment, she couldn't be sure.

"Uh, I'm not—"

"C'mon," the girl said, taking Erin's wrist and tugging her across the backyard.

The moment the girl's hand touched Erin's skin, Erin felt a warm, soothing feeling spread through her. It was comforting, but it was also dizzying. It felt a bit like the time Erin had caught the flu and she'd had a really high fever. When she'd been that sick, she'd been completely out of it, in a total daze.

"Where are we going?" Erin asked. Her voice sounded distant, even to her own ears, as the girl with the curly blonde hair pulled her along toward the house. The girl's steps crunched across the grass as the sound of the insects and birds faded into the background, like a soundtrack's volume being turned down.

"You'll see," the girl said with a giggle.

Normally, Erin would've hated that answer. She would've

yanked her hand away and refused to go another step with the strange, mysterious girl. But right now, she didn't much care. If anything, she was curious, almost a little excited, to see what the girl was going to show her.

The girl opened the back door to Erin's new house and hurried down the hallway, as if this were *her* house and not Erin's. Erin almost stopped her to remind the girl to take off her shoes at the back door, but the girl was moving too fast and Erin felt too hazy to do anything but simply follow.

As they passed through the hallway, Erin's gaze caught on a photograph hanging on the wall. It was one she'd never seen before, and she knew it definitely didn't belong to *her* family. For one, Erin's family was nowhere in it. The black-and-white photo was of complete strangers—well, with the exception of one face. The same blonde girl was in the photo . . . along with another blonde girl who looked exactly like her.

Twins? Erin thought, unconsciously slowing her steps to get a better look at the photo.

But the girl didn't let her. She tugged hard on Erin's arm, so hard it hurt. "Come *on*." The girl's voice was biting and fierce. Erin hurried to follow her, the girl's tone frightening.

The girl and Erin came to a stop at the entryway of the house, where the steps, the back hallway, the kitchen, and the entrance to the living room all came together. At the center of the floor were two paint cans that Erin didn't remember being there earlier. But then, they had been painting the house all week. It wasn't that strange to have two paint cans in the middle of the entryway, right?

With a finger to her lips, the girl smiled and bent down, grabbing a paintbrush sitting on the rim of the can. It dripped black paint down the handle.

Black? Erin hadn't remembered black paint anywhere in the house, yet here it was.

The girl took the paintbrush, dripping with liquid darkness, and smashed its black bristles against the pristine wall.

Erin gasped. Even dazed and bleary-eyed, she knew the action was wrong. Her parents would hate the black smear on their beautiful freshly painted cream-colored wall.

"What are you doing?" Erin whispered.

Instead of answering, the girl handed Erin the paintbrush, and moved around behind her. She took Erin by the shoulders and that same feeling of being lost in a daze quadrupled. It mingled with a warm, comforting sensation that made Erin feel like she was floating.

At the same time, a terrible feeling of wrongness pooled in her gut.

"Are you sure we should be doing this?" Erin asked.

Once again, the girl did not answer. She squeezed Erin's shoulders and Erin could no longer fight the strange urge. Erin slashed the paintbrush across the light cream canvas that was the wall. It left a terrible, crooked black smear about a foot long. It looked like a crack in the wall. A crack that led into a deep cave.

Erin felt another squeeze on her shoulders and heard a light giggle that raised the hairs on the back of her neck. Though she knew she shouldn't, she raked the paintbrush downward in a slant on the wall, touching the baseboards. Her breath let loose in that one stroke and she gasped again, sucking in another cold breath and that stung her lungs. It was like jumping into the pool when it was too cold out. The way the frigid air made her blood race to heat the rest of her body, creating a well of adrenaline she couldn't contain.

Erin flew up the steps with her paintbrush, making a long

jagged black line. Her feet pounded like drums, echoing up and down the stairs with the force of a hammer banging on wood. Then she swirled it and stabbed it, all the while black paint dribbled down the wall, down the paintbrush handle, and onto her hands. A black mark got on the hem of her T-shirt, and Erin didn't even think about how hard it would be to get out.

When she ran out of paint on her brush, she hurried back down the steps. The blonde girl was waiting for her, a bright smile on her face. Then, with one swift kick, the girl knocked over the open paint can. A sea of black oozed out of the can, gaining speed as it rushed across the surface of the wood.

Without a care in the world, the girl stepped into the black paint, holding out her hand for Erin to take.

Erin was panting. The cold was still in her lungs, and the adrenaline raced in her blood, but her skin felt warm and tingly. Her head was cloudy, but she knew she had to take the girl's hand. There was something telling her to. Compelling her to.

So she took the girl's hand and together, they stepped through the black pool of paint on the floor and walked down the hall, toward the back door, leaving a trail of black footprints.

Somewhere in the back of her head, Erin knew one thing. "My parents are going to be so mad."

At that, the curly-headed girl laughed, and turned to look at Erin over her shoulder. "If you never go back, you'll never have to worry about them."

Erin opened her mouth to ask what the girl meant, when the black paint under her shoes started expanding. Wider and wider the puddle of inky blackness grew. And before she realized it, her shoes were sinking into the darkness. Like quicksand, the black pool ate her shoes, and then her ankles, and then started up her calves and reached her knees.

A cold panic seared inside Erin, cutting through whatever warm, hazy feeling she'd had. She thrashed in the black ooze, trying to get out, but that only made it worse. So much worse. It reached her hips in no time at all, then her waist, and her chest and then her shoulders . . .

Erin raised her arms, reaching for something to hold on to, all while black ooze dripped onto her cheeks.

"Help!" she screamed above her at the blonde girl who still stood next to her, calm as ever. Her expression was cold. She said nothing, even as the black ooze reached Erin's chin.

Erin opened her mouth to scream again, but the liquid flooded past her lips, into her mouth, and so her scream became garbled. The ooze quickly swallowed her ears and silence dropped on her like a weight.

Then came a shout.

"ERIN!"

5

Erin jerked awake. She was panting, her heart thrumming loudly in her chest. Her skin felt like *ice*, even though it was covered in sweat.

But the shout still rang in her ears like a fire alarm's peal. Because it was so clear and loud, she could tell that it was her mother's voice. It was impressive, considering Erin was still in the treehouse.

Groaning, Erin sat up from her cramped, curled-up position on the hard floor, feeling stiff and uncomfortable. Not to mention, totally confused. Had that...all been a dream? The blonde-haired girl, the painting on the walls, and the black ooze that had almost drowned her...It had felt *so* real, but it was already beginning to fade into the back of her mind like a dream was supposed to do. The girl's appearance, the changes to the treehouse, the photograph on the wall, and the black paint—it was all becoming hard to recall the details. Everything from the strange dream slowly became shrouded in a bleak, cold fog. While she tried to remember what exactly had happened in the dream, she just couldn't.

And she was glad of it, because by the end, it had felt much more like a nightmare. Probably the most frightening she'd ever had.

"ERIN!"

Her mother's call echoed through the backyard and Erin gulped hard. Her mother didn't shout, or she didn't like to, so the fact that she'd yelled twice in that last minute couldn't mean anything good.

Without packing up any of her things, Erin hurriedly climbed down from the treehouse and raced across the backyard. The sun had already dried up a good bit of the mud from last night, so it wasn't quite as wet in the grass. Still, she kicked off her shoes on the porch and entered the house in nothing but her socks.

She was met right at the door by her mother, looking downright furious.

"What were you *thinking*, Erin?" Mrs. Dodgeson said through clenched teeth. Her hands were at her side, balled into fists. A red flush was creeping up her neck under her curtain of dark hair.

Erin was dumbfounded. She had no idea what to say as she took in the sight of her mother, so rarely angry. Her mother was always the picture of calm and peace, even the time when Becca had ruined her favorite rug by spilling an entire cup of pudding all over it. It was in Mrs. Dodgeson's nature to seek to understand rather than accuse. It was what she told Erin over and over when Becca made a mess of things, as she so often did.

"Um, I—I don't..." Erin stuttered.

Her mother's eyes flashed as she stepped back and pointed down the hall. "Go to the stairs. Tell me what you see."

This is a test, Erin thought.

Of course her mother already knew what was there—she didn't need to be told anything. A feeling of absolute dread pooled in Erin's stomach as she walked down the hall, her mother at her heels. Along with that dread came a scattering of goose bumps that crept down Erin's spine.

When Erin finally got to the entryway, and the foot of the

stairs, she didn't need to look hard at all to find out what had her mother so enraged. All along the newly painted wall were thick, black scribbles, starting at the bottom of the steps and going up. At Erin's feet was the same black permanent marker she had used to label the boxes after breakfast.

Someone had taken the black marker and drawn—no, scrawled—all over the wall.

And Mom thinks I did it.

Erin looked back at her mother, who towered behind her, arms folded, eyes narrowed. It didn't take a genius to figure out that her mother blamed her.

"It . . . it wasn't me!" Erin said. "I left the marker on the boxes, maybe Becca—"

"*Erin.*" Mrs. Dodgeson's voice was tight with frustration. Erin could tell she was struggling to refrain from yelling. "Your sister has been in her room the whole time, singing and working on her puzzle. I can't believe you're blaming her for something *you* obviously did."

Erin hated that her mother would think her capable of something so childish, not to mention destructive. "Mom! I didn't do this. I swear, I—"

Mrs. Dodgeson held up a hand to stop her. Then she pointed at the floor, her finger moving down the hall toward the back door. "Your footprints tell a different story."

At first, Erin was confused. She had taken off her shoes on the porch. But then she saw them. Muddy footprints on the shiny hardwood floor coming down the hall, then going up the steps, and then returning to the back door.

Erin's stomach sank while an icy cold chill crept up her body, starting at the soles of her feet. Those did look like her shoe prints, and it *had* been muddy when she walked to the treehouse that morning.

But . . . but . . .

The cold feeling in her limbs and creeping up her chest reminded her of the iciness in her lungs during that strange dream. The adrenaline coursing through her as she raced up the stairs with a paintbrush drenched in black. Slathering the walls in black paint in almost the exact same strokes as the permanent marker.

Erin sucked in a breath.

Oh my gosh, she thought as her heart pounded hard in the chest. *The dream! It's just like it! Only with a marker instead of a brush.*

Erin swallowed and stared, stunned, at the wall covered in black squiggles. How much of it had been a dream, and how much of it had been reality?

"Honestly, Erin," her mother said, her shoulders sagging with a heavy sigh. "I just can't fathom why you'd do this."

Erin didn't answer. She didn't know what to say. Nothing—*nothing*—made sense. There was no way Erin would've done this in her right mind, fully awake and fully aware. She remembered how in the dream she'd been in a daze, confused, not entirely *there*. She remembered how that blonde girl had handed her the paintbrush, taken her shoulders, and . . .

"Was last week too much for you?"

Erin blinked, looking back up at her mother.

Gone was the anger and frustration. Mrs. Dodgeson had adopted her gentle, understanding face and voice. The voice Erin had sometimes heard her use when talking to her clients—other children and their parents who were undergoing "issues that needed special attention," as her mother liked to refer to it.

"I know we worked very hard last week," her mother started slowly. "There was a lot to clean, and so much painting to do. I understand if you were tired or frustrated. But *this*"—she gestured to the thick black scribbles on the wall—"is no way to tell me. You need to use your words."

Erin bit her bottom lip. She wanted to argue. To tell her mother that it wasn't too much work. She hadn't been acting out at all. In fact, she'd been just as eager as her mother about cleaning and unpacking. She wanted this new house to feel like home as quickly as possible. Why would she ruin all that effort by doing something as silly as scribbling on the wall?

But it's no use, Erin thought defeatedly. There were too many signs that pointed to her as the culprit. The muddy shoe prints, for one, and for another, well, who else could it have been if not for Becca or herself?

Erin immediately remembered the girl from the treehouse. She'd kept telling herself that it had been a trick of the shadows, but what if it hadn't? What if she'd been right the first time and there really *had* been a girl there? Somehow the girl could've snuck into the house, through the back door, wearing Erin's shoes and drawn all over the wall.

Erin's shoulders slumped. *No, even that sounds too far-fetched.*

As her mother launched into a long lecture about caring about other people's property and using words to explain feelings, not actions, Erin couldn't help but grow more frustrated. Her hands balled into fists that clutched the hem of her shirt.

That's when she saw it.

Something that made Erin's skin grow just as chilled as when she was up in the treehouse.

There was a black mark on the edge of her T-shirt. A stain that she remembered getting while painting in the dream. It was thick and dark and in the exact. Same. Spot.

Oh no . . .

Erin folded her hand over the mark, squeezing the edge of her shirt, hoping it would disappear.

There was a chance she could've accidentally marked her T-shirt while labeling the boxes, but Erin knew with absolute certainty that she hadn't. She would've remembered, and she would've been irritated about it. There were so few of her shirts and clothes that Becca hadn't spilled on or messed up in some way. Plus, what were the chances that it would've been in the exact same spot as in her dream?

With a shaking hand, Erin released her shirt. The stain was still there. And maybe it would never come out.

"Erin? Are you listening?" her mother asked with a tired sigh.

"Yes," Erin answered, though she hadn't been.

"Go up to your room. We'll repaint the wall tomorrow."

Unable to look at her mother and see the obvious disappointment on her face, Erin turned on her heel and headed upstairs. Her thoughts were a tangle of contradictory certainties and doubts. She was certain she would've never purposely written on the wall. But she doubted that it could've been anyone else. She was certain that the paint and the blonde girl had all been a dream. Except she doubted that the mysterious girl from the treehouse was *just* a dream.

At the top of the stairs, a light giggle whispered next to her ear. *Psst.*

Erin whirled around, cupping her ear, her heart racing. What was *that*?

As her socked foot pivoted on the hardwood floor, she slipped on the edge of the step. She very nearly fell, but managed to grab the staircase railing before it was too late. She did bang her knee though, and that *really* hurt.

"Erin!" her mother called. "Are you all right?"

Pulse pounding, knee stinging, Erin scurried into her room feeling like a mouse being chased by a cat. "I'm fine!" she called to her mother. But the lie tasted bitter in her mouth and the goose bumps on her skin showed no sign of fading, even in the heat of her bedroom warmed by the summer sun.

6

Erin lay on her bed, face turned toward the wall of her room. She couldn't focus on any books, and her mother had taken her phone and her game console, so she couldn't play anything either. She wasn't tired, not after her long nap, but part of her wished she *could* fall asleep. Mostly she wanted to shut her brain off and stop thinking about the scribbled-on wall, the strange dream-turned-nightmare, the mystery girl, and her mother's rage.

The other part of her didn't want to fall asleep in case it happened again.

Unfortunately, she kept replaying the events in her mind and grew more and more frustrated that certain details kept slipping from her memories like sand through her fingers. It felt so much like a dream in that way. How they would fade the moment you started to wake up. Erin struggled to hold on to specifics, like the girl grabbing her shoulders or handing her the paintbrush. Or like the fact the treehouse had looked different—newer, somehow.

At one point, Becca had knocked on Erin's door, asking her to play, but Mrs. Dodgeson told Becca that Erin was in a timeout. Erin was also pretty sure her mother had raised her voice when inviting Becca to go downstairs and bake cookies instead.

Erin just rolled her eyes. *Okay, I get it, I'm being punished.*

But did she actually deserve it? Never mind what her mother thought. What did Erin, herself, think? Did she think she'd really done it? Even with the footprints and the stain on her shirt? She wanted to say no—that it had all been just one big misunderstanding or something—but the truth was ...

When Erin closed her eyes, and really thought about it, instead of the paintbrush, she could actually feel the grip of the marker in her hand. She could remember the pressure she made, gliding the marker over the pristine, freshly painted wall.

Maybe *that* was what really scared her. The fact that somewhere, buried deep in her mind, was the memory that she actually *had* done it. Only she didn't know how or for what reason, or even why she couldn't remember it.

It was both frustrating and terrifying.

Erin stayed in her room through lunch and well into the late afternoon. It wasn't until her empty stomach growled loudly that she decided to seek out food. Her father was in the kitchen, preparing pasta, and he gave her a little smile and ruffle of her hair. Hopefully her parents thought that she'd been punished enough.

Becca leapt from her seat at the kitchen table, where she'd been coloring once again, and zoomed over to Erin. She threw her small thin arms around Erin's waist. "Erin! I missed you!" she cried, in her loud, somewhat annoying, voice.

But Erin found she didn't mind it this time. The warm hug and affection from her little sister actually made Erin feel a little guilty for trying to blame the wall scribbling on Becca. Becca messed up a lot of things, ruined toys and clothes, but it was never on purpose. And she looked up to Erin too much to try to get her in trouble.

Dinner wasn't as tense as it could've been. Her mother seemed to have cooled down after several hours, and she spent the majority of the meal talking about ideas for her next book. As Erin listened to her mother talk about the effects of children being overworked and stressed, Erin knew that the "wall incident" (which was what Mrs. Dodgeson was now calling it) had been her mother's inspiration.

Erin tried not to let it bother her. At least it wasn't another lecture. She just stuffed her mouth with pasta and chewed, thinking about a science fiction novel she wanted to read after dinner. It was then she remembered that she'd brought the book up into the treehouse.

The *treehouse.*

Erin couldn't stop the feeling of chills tingling up her spine at the thought of it. Yes, it was just a treehouse. A super-cool, fun treehouse, but wasn't that where all the weirdness had begun? And hadn't that neighbor girl, Tara, told her very clearly not to go up into it? Could her warning actually have been *for real*? She couldn't help but replay Tara's warning in her head:

"I would . . . stay out of it. Like, seriously.*"*

It seemed silly to believe in any weird rumors, especially from other kids who loved to scare and exaggerate. Then again . . . it was the treehouse that had captured Becca's attention and made her so scared that she wouldn't even go into it. It was the tree-house where the mystery girl had first appeared, framed in the window. And it was the treehouse where Erin had first fallen asleep and had that strange dream, which seemed to have gotten her into all that trouble.

As Erin stirred the pasta around on her plate, she thought, *I'm being stupid. It's just a treehouse. That's all.*

And yet . . . Erin didn't *want* to go back inside. Her gut was telling her not to. At least, not tonight. Maybe her dad could get the book for her later.

After dinner, Erin did the dishes, which seemed to win some points in her favor. Her mother kissed the top of her head and ruffled her hair just as her father had done.

"There's my good girl," Mrs. Dodgeson said affectionately.

With the day's events well behind her, Erin headed back up to her room, got ready for bed, and slipped under the covers. It took her longer to fall asleep than usual, but eventually she got drowsy enough that the last thing she remembered looking at was the old globe she'd unpacked from the boxes and had left on her desk.

A scratching, tapping sound woke Erin up in the middle of the night. At first, it sounded like someone was in the walls, raking at the wood with long fingernails—causing Erin's breath to catch in her throat. But then the light from the moon illuminated the dark branches and leaves that scraped against the glass in her window. Erin let out a relieved sigh and settled back into her covers. Calmly, she watched the leaves flutter and press against the window as the night breeze carried through their backyard.

Erin didn't get scared very easily. Mrs. Dodgeson had always bragged about this while Erin was growing up. Erin didn't think there were monsters under her bed, or in her closets, and she didn't believe in ghosts or spirits. Living in Chicago, in a city where she learned to be wary of the bustling traffic and strangers on the street, she just didn't have room to be scared of the supernatural.

So, when the old globe on her desk started to rotate slowly on its own, issuing a soft creak, Erin didn't think much of it. It was the blow of the air conditioner fan into her room, moving the globe. That was all.

Still, the sight was a little creepy.

The world spun slowly on its brass axis, turning, inch by inch, showing the Pacific Ocean, the Pacific Islands, Japan, Russia, all of Asia. Then it started to spin a little faster and the creaking grew louder.

"Well, that's annoying," Erin announced to her empty room as she threw back her covers. She crossed to her desk, stopped the globe with her fingers, and put her other hand out to feel the breeze causing the globe to spin.

But there was nothing. Not from a crack at the window, nor from an air-conditioning vent.

Frowning, Erin stared at the globe, then removed her fingers. The globe stayed still.

"Maybe a screw is loose," Erin muttered to herself as she inspected the axis of the globe. She couldn't find anything, but that didn't mean it wasn't there. With a shrug, Erin turned back toward her bed.

Halfway there, the doorknob of her bedroom turned.

Erin froze.

"Becca?" she asked.

There was no response.

She wasn't surprised her little sister was visiting her room.

The first few nights in the new house, Becca hadn't slept well alone, so Erin had let her sleep in her bed. Though recently, Becca had seemed to grow used to her own room and had been sleeping alone. But maybe something had spooked her. Like the branches on the window in Erin's own room.

"Becca? You can come in," Erin whispered, moving to the door and grabbing the doorknob and pulling the door open.

Becca wasn't there. *No* one was there. The hallway was empty except for shadows.

Erin stood there, staring at nothing for a few long seconds. The doorknob had turned, hadn't it? She hadn't imagined that. She'd seen the movement, heard the very faint squeak.

Now the hairs on the back of her neck were standing to attention, pulling her skin tight with nerves. Just what was going on in her room? Or worse, her mind?

Erin stepped back and shut the door, staring at the doorknob.

Just when she was about to return to bed, the doorknob turned again slowly. Right before her eyes.

With a gasp, Erin grabbed the knob, wrenched it open, and was about to yell at Becca for playing a prank—but stopped.

No one was there again. She poked her head outside the door and looked up and down the hall. No one.

"What's going on?" Erin breathed. Real fear was starting to creep up her spine. It stretched into her limbs and through her blood, reaching her heart and making it pound.

Erin closed the door and then, to her horror, the doorknob started to rattle and shake. Before, the movement had been controlled and slow, but now it seemed like someone was on the other side of the door, desperately trying to get inside.

With a whimper, she stumbled and fell on her backside. The rattling became so violent, it shook the door in its frame.

Erin didn't scare easily. But this terrified her.

And she couldn't stop the cry that wrenched from her as the doorknob shook so hard it vibrated. "MOM! DAD!"

The moment the shout left her throat, the door stopped its shaking and the knob stopped its rattling. Seconds later, Erin heard pounding footsteps racing down the hall.

The door burst open and her father was in the doorway, wide-eyed and his short hair sticking up in every direction. Her mother stood behind him, looking like she'd just been in the middle of a deep sleep as well.

"Erin? What? What is it?" her father asked, looking around her room.

Erin still sat on the floor, frozen in place. She looked up at her parents and opened and closed her mouth.

What could she say that didn't sound like she'd made the whole thing up? Even *she* didn't believe what she'd just witnessed. So how could she convince her parents that an invisible something or someone had been trying to get into her bedroom? She'd already got in a load of trouble that day, she didn't want her parents thinking that she was making up stories for attention.

Finally, she lied. "I . . . had a bad dream."

Her father's shoulders sagged. Her mother sighed heavily. They looked both relieved and slightly annoyed. Only a bad dream.

While Mrs. Dodgeson went downstairs to get Erin a glass of warm milk, Mr. Dodgeson sat next to Erin on the floor beside her bed.

"Do you want to tell me about it, sweetheart?" her father asked.

Erin just shook her head. It was bad enough she was lying in the first place, she didn't want to have to pile more lies on top.

Her father drew an arm around her shoulders and she snuggled into his side. Normally she wasn't so clingy, but today had been weird, stressful, and a little ... frightening.

"You know a dream can't hurt you, right, Erin?" Mr. Dodgeson said gently.

Erin nodded, not trusting herself to speak. If she did, she might tell her dad everything. About hearing whispers, the door rattling with no one behind it, and of course, the strange dream of painting on the wall with the mysterious blonde girl.

And when she thought about that nightmare, where the black ooze had almost swallowed her whole, she couldn't help but disagree with her dad.

Dreams *could* hurt you.

7

Erin headed down to breakfast the next morning, feeling drained and tired. She felt even worse when she saw the black scribbles on the wall and was reminded that *she* had somehow done those. Without reason or purpose. Just from the influence of one very awful nightmare.

Her heart gave a fearful lurch when she noticed paint cans at the bottom of the stairs—like from her dream. It wasn't black paint though, just the off-white hue that her mother had painted the rest of the walls with.

Carefully she side-stepped them and hurried into the kitchen for breakfast. Her father had already eaten and was in his new office, working. Becca was munching happily on some oatmeal, the TV from the living room blaring her favorite kids' show, and she was absorbed in it. Mrs. Dodgeson spooned a bowlful of oatmeal for Erin and set it in front of her.

"Hurry up and eat, hon," her mother said, taking a sip from her favorite coffee mug. It was a ceramic mug that Becca had painted in one of her kindergarten classes for Mother's Day. "Then we can get started on repainting your little art project."

Again, Erin wanted to scream, *I didn't do it!* But that wasn't exactly true. It seemed that she *had* done it. But not on *purpose*. What would her mother say to her if she'd done it because she was sleepwalking? That would probably open a can of worms that would just make matters worse. So instead she stuffed a spoonful of oatmeal in her mouth to stop herself from saying anything she'd regret.

After breakfast, Erin and Mrs. Dodgeson laid down a tarp on the stairs and repainted the marked-up areas of the walls. It took several coats of paint to cover the thick black lines, so they had to wait until one coat was dry to add the second. When it was all finally painted over, it was around time for lunch. So Mrs. Dodgeson fixed Erin and Becca grilled cheese sandwiches and then headed up to her office to work the rest of the afternoon.

Tired and full of grilled cheese, Erin was in no mood to go

outside and explore, so she let Becca turn on her TV show. The show wasn't all that interesting (it was made for five-year-olds), and in no time, Erin found herself nodding off.

When she opened her eyes again, Erin didn't recognize the living room. It was the same room for sure though. The front door was identical, the windows, the hardwood floor, the beams on the ceiling—all the same. But the furniture was different. Definitely not her family's. The couch she was sitting on was floral and stiff. The armchair was made of corduroy that was a deep maroon. The curtains that hung from the window were white with daisies embroidered on them. And the TV was . . . old. Like TVs that her grandparents had in photographs.

Slowly, Erin got to her feet, feeling tingles race down her spine. Something was wrong. Something like this had happened before, but she couldn't remember any details. Her head was foggy, and she was so tired even though she had just taken a nap.

"Mom?" she asked into the empty, unfamiliar living room. "Dad? Becca?"

No one answered. Frowning, Erin looked around more closely, hoping to recognize something familiar. Anything. Her gaze snagged on a photograph in a gilded frame, set on the side mahogany table next to the couch. Curious, Erin bent down to take a look.

Two identical twin girls were in the photo. Blonde, pretty, and smiling. One held a teddy bear in her arms, and the other one had her arm wrapped around her twin's shoulders. They stood under a large oak tree that looked vaguely familiar.

"Who's Becca?"

Erin whirled around. A girl with curly blonde hair stood next to the couch, right behind Erin. The girl had blue eyes, rosy cheeks, and a frilly pink dress. Erin glanced at the photo in the gold frame, back to the girl. It was her, one of the twins.

In the back of Erin's mind, a whisper told her that she should know this girl. More than just someone from an old photo. She'd met her before. Played with her before. But Erin just couldn't remember.

"Becca is..." Erin began, then trailed off. Her heartbeat stumbled as she realized she didn't know who this Becca was. "She's my..." Erin tried again, but her mind came up blank.

The girl tilted her head in confusion. "You're acting really strange."

Before Erin could respond, the girl straightened up with a

bright smile on her face. "Oh! I have something to show you. It's the bee's knees."

Bee's knees? Erin hadn't heard that expression before, and she was going to ask what it meant when the girl leaned over and grabbed Erin by the wrist. A familiar—but not—sensation traveled up Erin's arm. She was chilly and hot all at once, while the living room turned hazy. It was like someone dragged their hands on a wet oil painting, making all the colors smear. Once more, she felt like she was floating. A surreal, lovely feeling that she couldn't put into words.

The girl led Erin around the couch and into the kitchen. "I found it in our treehouse." The girl's voice was fast and airy with excitement. Her enthusiasm was contagious as she passed Erin a large mason jar with leaves, blades of grass, and twigs. And Erin found herself smiling as well, eager to take the jar. "I caught it and put it in this jar. We can bring it to show-and-tell at school. Swell, ain't it?"

Curious about what was inside, Erin lifted the jar up and peered at the bottom.

Against the glass, under the green leaves, was a big black spider.

Erin shrieked and dropped the glass jar. It shattered on the kitchen floor. Shards of glass, leaves, and twigs scattered across the linoleum. Then, not just one but *hundreds* of black spiders started scuttling from the remnants of the broken jar. They flooded across the floor and climbed up the walls and over Erin's shoes.

Shrieking, she started dancing and kicking away at the spiders. But more followed. It felt like a thousand little legs were roaming up and down her skin. At any moment, she expected the bites to come. Unable to watch the spiders crawl up any farther, Erin slammed her eyes shut as a strangled cry escaped her lips.

With a gasp, Erin lurched forward—off the couch's pillows and out of the terrible nightmare. She nearly fell to the floor and almost collided with the coffee table.

Heart pounding, Erin looked all around the living room. It was back to their own furniture and their sleek flat-screen TV.

Another nightmare? It had to have been, because already the details were beginning to slip from her grasp. She struggled to hold on to them. The blonde girl had been back, invading her dream and saying strange things. Who was this girl and why did she feel so familiar?

Though she wasn't sure why, she looked to her left at the couch's end table. The old photograph of the twin girls was missing. No...it had never been there in the first place. It had been part of the dream, but she wanted to remember it because somehow she knew it was important.

As Erin's heartbeat started to calm, she realized that Becca's kids' show was still playing on TV, but Becca was nowhere to be seen. Had she gone up to her room while Erin had been asleep? A little worried, Erin headed toward the stairs to check on her little sister when something caught her eye on the kitchen floor.

For one terrifying moment, Erin had the image of the big black spider—then *hundreds* of them—but it wasn't that at all. It was a large shard of blue ceramic. Erin sucked in a breath as she stepped into the kitchen.

"Oh no," Erin muttered as she stared at her mother's favorite coffee mug all across the kitchen floor in pieces.

As Erin tried to figure how it could've been broken, and what to do next, footsteps came behind her. A sharp gasp cut through Erin's worries and she turned around to find her mother in the hall, gaze locked on her beloved shattered mug.

"Erin...what..." Mrs. Dodgeson looked stricken. Her eyebrows were pulled together and her lips were turned down in a deep frown. "Did you...break this?"

Erin had to think fast. Her first instinct was to tell her mother it had been Becca, because Erin knew it hadn't been herself, of course. She would never have dropped her mom's favorite mug, at least, not on purpose. But suggesting it was Becca hadn't gone so well yesterday with the "wall incident." Not to mention, she'd seen her mother wash the mug that morning after breakfast. Saw her put it away in the cupboard... and Becca couldn't reach the cupboard.

So it couldn't have been Becca either. Who could it have been? Her dad? Unlikely.

"Erin?" her mother prodded. Sadness was in Mrs. Dodgeson's eyes. After all, it was a precious mug her youngest daughter had painted for her.

Around the corner of the hall, Erin caught a glimpse of blonde hair. Erin's stomach dropped as goose bumps ran across her chilled skin. The blonde girl from the dream. The jar with the spider shattering in the kitchen. Had Erin been holding a jar . . . or a ceramic mug? Like last time, the details of the dream were starting to fade, and all she could really remember were the emotions that gripped her. The *fear* being the strongest of all.

Tears started to prick Erin's eyes. In addition to the fear, confusion grabbed hold of her, making her chest tight and hard to breathe.

What's happening to me?

"Oh, Erin . . ." her mother said with a sigh. Clearly Mrs. Dodgeson had taken the look on Erin's face to be an admission of guilt. And it was, a little bit. Because Erin had done something *again* that she hadn't meant to do—hadn't had any control over doing. And that was the scariest thing of all.

How could she tell her mother that a blonde girl in her dreams was tricking her into doing all these things? It sounded ridiculous!

"It was an accident," Erin finally said after she'd managed to control the shake in her voice. *That*, at least, was the truth.

"I'm sure it was, sweetie," her mother said kindly, but there was no mistaking the deep disappointment. "Why don't you get the broom from the closet and we'll clean this up?"

"O-okay," Erin said meekly. With her gaze on the corner where she'd seen the blonde hair, Erin headed into the hallway toward the closet where they kept coats and cleaning supplies. Instead of seeing the mystery girl, she found Becca sitting on the steps in the middle of the stairs. As soon as Becca saw Erin though, her eyes grew wide, and she raced up the steps and into her bedroom. The door shut with a bang.

Erin had no idea what to make of her sister's reaction. It was almost like she was *scared* of Erin.

"Hurry, Erin. I don't want anyone stepping on these shards," Mrs. Dodgeson called.

With what felt like a thousand pounds on her shoulders, Erin slumped to the closet and grabbed the broom.

～⤙

Erin never had so much trouble sleeping in her life. She seemed to wake up in the middle of the night at every little sound. The branches hitting the window, the creak of the stairs, the squeak of the floorboards, even the wind outside. The following day, she tried to tell her father about the noises, but he just told her it was all a part of living in a house and not a big city.

"But there's no more car alarms or sirens down the street,

right?" Mr. Dodgeson said patiently over breakfast. "Don't worry, hon, you'll get used to it."

Not fast enough, Erin thought irritably as she pushed the scrambled eggs around on her plate.

She was going to be tired again that day, but this time, she refused to fall asleep. Whatever was happening with her dreams and her sleepwalking, it seemed that it snuck up on her when she took a nap during the day. To make sure she didn't fall asleep, Erin took Becca outside and the two played jump rope, hopscotch, and drew colorful scenes of unicorns, rainbows, and dragons with sidewalk chalk on their driveway. It must've worked, because the day went by without any strange incidents.

Even better, Erin was so exhausted that she slept soundly through the night without being woken up by a single noise. A few days went by and Erin believed the strange dreams, the sleepwalking, and the blonde mystery girl were all behind her.

One afternoon, a full week after her visit to the treehouse, Erin was reading her new issue of *National Geographic* (it had come in the mail just that morning) out on the porch. It was a beautiful summer day. Warm, but pleasant, thanks to the breeze and the shade of the awning. She was so comfortable in the rocking chair that she must've dozed off.

While she was sleeping, she dreamed of running water. A babbling brook with ripples that shined in the sunlight and smooth pebbles that sparkled under the clear water. She imagined dipping her fingers in the cool water and heard the high-pitched laughs of a girl over the sound of the water rushing across the rocks.

It was so peaceful that she felt happy and content. Like she could stay playing in the creek, with the sunlight and the minnows, forever.

"Isn't this lovely?" a voice whispered next to her ear. *"You could stay here forever,"* the voice continued, echoing her thoughts.

Before Erin could reply that forever was a long time, a stuffed teddy bear was pushed into her arms. But it was sopping wet. As if it had been *drowned* or fished out from the creek. An icy feeling spread through her limbs at the feel of the toy in her arms.

Then a roll of thunder shook the ground under Erin's feet.

BOOM.

It was so loud that it made Erin's teeth clack together. Driving rain hit the creek's water, splashing with so much force that it looked like the sea caught in a storm. A wave hit Erin in the side, knocking her to her hands and knees as another clap of thunder echoed not just above her, but all around her.

Then a sudden bolt of lightning hit the creek, illuminating the darkness that had descended. Revealing a small blonde-haired figure in the waves . . .

"WHOA!"

A shout jerked Erin awake and out of her rocking chair. She gasped like she'd been caught swimming for her life in that storm.

"ERIN! Get in here NOW."

This time it was her father yelling from inside the house. Erin was still trembling from the impact of the lightning strike within her dream, and the icy chill of the waves that had crashed against her. But as she struggled to remember the rest of the dream, once again, it started to slip away.

Beyond frustrated, and with a terrible feeling of dread, Erin rushed into the house, where she found her father in the kitchen.

He was standing next to the sink, which was overflowing with water.

Erin could do nothing but stare in shock as her father grabbed dish towels from the drawer and tossed them on the floor, mopping up puddles that had started running into the hallway. Soapy water had flowed out of the full sink and down the cupboards to pool on the floor.

"Don't just stand there. Go get more towels, Erin," Mr. Dodgeson snapped as he unplugged the sink so it could start draining.

Erin swallowed thickly and turned on her heel. She ran up the stairs to the bathroom she shared with Becca and grabbed armfuls of towels. By the time she'd made it back down to the kitchen, her mother was already there with a mop. Her parents looked annoyed, but they said nothing as they took the towels from Erin, dropped them to the flooded floor, and soaked up the remaining water.

It wasn't until they took the dripping towels outside to wring them out that her father turned to her. "Erin, did you forget to turn off the water after you did the dishes?"

Erin had suspected this was coming. It was true that it had

been her job to wash the dishes after lunch, but she had turned off the water. She was *sure* of it.

She shook her head. "No, I turned it off. I remember doing it."

"Erin . . ." Her father took a deep breath. "Becca is too short to reach the sink. It had to have been you."

Erin wanted to point out that she hadn't even mentioned it could've been Becca. Only that *she* hadn't done it.

"But I swear! I did the dishes, went outside to read, and then fell . . . asleep . . ." A cold feeling spread through Erin's chest and down her spine as she said the words.

She'd fallen asleep. Again. And something bad had happened. Again.

She desperately tried to recall certain moments from her dream. There *had* been running water in her dream. A creek. Could her mind have replaced the water in the sink with the water from the creek? Just like the paintbrush and the permanent marker? The mason jar and the coffee mug? She tried to prove her hunch wrong, but she remembered dipping her fingers into the cold creek water, and if she thought about it—*really* thought about it—she remembered her fingers clutching the silver handles of the faucet.

Or had they? The pleasant dream of the creek had quickly morphed into a nightmare with thunder and lightning and waves that threatened to pull her under. She couldn't be sure of anything more than the panic and desperation of the nightmare.

She just didn't know. It was terrifying—questioning what was real, and what wasn't.

Erin's father leaned over her, squeezing her shoulder gently. "Erin, you're going to have to be more careful. This is our home now, that we own. We have to take care of our property. Do you understand?"

Erin curled her hands into fists as she just nodded along to her dad's lecture. Apparently whatever was happening to her was not done at all. In fact, she wondered if it was just beginning.

8

It was that haunting thought that kept Erin up well past midnight. She stared at the clock in her bedroom, willing herself to fall asleep, but she was wide awake. Of course, it didn't help that she'd had a nap that afternoon.

"It's no use," Erin finally grumbled.

Frustrated, Erin sat up and threw the covers aside, got out of bed, and marched over to her door. Just before she was about to grab the doorknob, she paused, thinking about a week ago where it had moved and shook on its own. It hadn't happened since, but she still thought about it a lot. What had made the doorknob turn? Or *who*?

Erin opened the door and stepped out into the hall. She couldn't help looking around, squinting into the corners where the shadows were the darkest. Something in the back of her mind told her to. Like the other night, the hall was empty. She was still on edge though, and passing by the bathroom just made her nerves jump higher. Erin caught her reflection in the bathroom mirror. Her pale face, lit only by the moonlight coming in from the hall window, stared back at her. Her reflection looked frightened. Unsure.

It wasn't normal for Erin. She hated feeling this way. She'd always been independent and capable. Feeling vulnerable and scared definitely wasn't something she was used to.

With a deep breath, she headed downstairs for a glass of water. After triple-checking that the water from the faucet was turned off, she made her way back up the steps.

She was walking past the bathroom when a voice whispered right in her ear.

Psst.

Erin jumped, whipping toward the direction of the whisper. "Wh-who's there?"

Just like that time at the top of the stairs, where she'd heard something similar, no one was actually there. But there was no mistaking the feeling of breath on her neck. The tickling of her hair as it brushed against her cheek, like someone had moved it to whisper in her ear.

Erin's heart thumped loudly in her chest.

Paula . . .

This time it came from her other side, and she jerked around, toward the voice. What she saw made her gasp and drop her water glass. The glass cracked and rolled across the floor, cold water splashing across Erin's toes and soaking the bottom of her feet.

In the bathroom mirror was the girl with the blonde curls.

Erin recognized her immediately. She'd seen the girl's profile once in the treehouse, and now twice in her dreams. But this was the first time that her features were clear and not shrouded by shadows. The girl stared out from the mirror at Erin with a cold, vacant gaze. Her skin was deathly—no, *ghostly*—pale, and pulled tight across the bones of her face. It made her cheeks look sharp and sunken. Her blonde curls weren't shiny or bouncy—they hung limp and stringy around her shoulders. She wore a faded nightgown and her lips were an icy blue.

As she gawked back at the girl in the reflection of the mirror,

Erin found she couldn't move. Prickles of coldness started to pinch Erin's skin and sharp stabs of fear poked her between the ribs.

"Wh-who are you?" Erin asked. She'd seen this girl in her dreams, but also somewhere else. A photo? There had been two of her in the photo. Twins. Was that right? Erin didn't know anymore. She couldn't be sure of anything—especially any details from her dreams.

The girl said nothing. She just continued to stare at Erin with those lifeless eyes. It was more than unsettling. It was haunting.

Erin wanted to turn and run away, but she knew without a shadow of a doubt that this girl was behind everything.

Am I dreaming again?

It was entirely possible. This girl had only showed up in her dreams and so she couldn't help but worry—was this all just another terrible nightmare?

With a hard swallow, Erin stepped into the bathroom, lifting her hand to turn on the light. As she lifted her hand, so too did the blonde girl. Her movement was the exact same as Erin's. The same time, the same position. It was a mirror reflection.

Blood pounding hard in her ears, Erin's fingers trembled as they tapped against the wall, trying to find the light switch. Her eyes couldn't leave the girl's. It was if she was trapped by them, held captive by their cold depths.

"Erin?"

Erin gasped and jumped back out into the hall.

Becca was there in her unicorn night shirt, clutching Mr. Fuzzy Hooves to her chest. Her bedroom door was open and she was rubbing her eyes and yawning, as if she'd just woken up.

Erin glanced back at the bathroom mirror. The girl had vanished. Erin's own frightened reflection had returned.

"Are you really . . . Erin?" Becca asked softly.

At Becca's words, Erin tore her gaze from the mirror and stared in surprise at her little sister. What did she mean by that? "Of course I am. Who else would I be?"

Becca bit her bottom lip and hugged her stuffed giraffe to her chest. It was obvious the little girl didn't want to say anything else.

"Becca," Erin started, taking a step toward her sister, "you have to tell me. What—"

The door to her parents' bedroom opened just then and their dad appeared at the threshold, looking exhausted.

"Girls?" Mr. Dodgeson said in a yawn as he looked from Erin to Becca. "What's going on? What are you two doing up? I thought I heard something."

Mr. Dodgeson frowned when he saw the cracked glass and the water all across the hall. "What happened here?"

Erin looked down at the mess. She hadn't even noticed it. Seeing the girl in the mirror had truly scared her. She'd never been so freaked out in her life. But even now, she didn't want to tell her parents the truth. For one, she knew they wouldn't believe her. For another, she didn't want to admit how scared she really was. Her mother would ask how she was feeling five hundred times a day, and her father would just baby her.

Not to mention that admitting this was all happening out loud would make it . . . real.

"I—I stubbed my toe," Erin lied. "It was dark, and I accidentally dropped my glass of water."

Mr. Dodgeson helped her wipe up the water and then he tucked Becca back into bed.

Erin went into her room, and, with a shiver crawling up her spine, she ducked her head under the covers.

"You're not real," Erin whispered to herself in the quiet. "You're a dream. That's all."

Because admitting she was being haunted by a ghost would be worse than any nightmare.

9

After another night of very little sleep, Erin knew she had to make sure that what she'd told herself over and over again the night before was true—that the blonde girl was nothing more than a figment of her imagination, or someone who only appeared in her dreams.

Not a ... ghost.

It was hard for her to even think that being haunted by a ghost was an actual possibility. Up until a few days ago, she hadn't believed that ghosts actually existed. But that girl in the mirror ... how else could Erin explain her appearance? The girl had looked *dead*. Like a walking corpse. And how could the girl have been *inside* the mirror copying Erin's movements?

Erin wanted to believe it was all just one bad dream after another. She knew minds could do strange things. But she didn't know how to prove it other than to wait for another awful thing to happen. She just kept thinking and *thinking* about everything that had happened and how it was all connected: The blonde girl, the photos where there were *two* of her, the letter *P*, the treehouse.

Although it had been a long time since she'd gone to the treehouse, she thought back to what Tara, the neighbor girl, had said over a week and a half ago. Tara had obviously been trying to warn her of something bad. Had it been a ghost? Had her going into the treehouse somehow triggered this haunting? That *had* been where she'd seen the blonde girl first, after all.

Unfortunately she didn't know where Tara lived to go and ask her for more details about the possible haunting. And she obviously couldn't go up and down their street knocking on strangers' doors, looking for her.

There was one thing that she could think to do, but she didn't want to. It was almost like admitting that something was really and truly wrong. It had to do with what Becca had said to her in the hallway last night.

"Are you really Erin?"

It freaked Erin out. Why would Becca ask her that question?

Who else could she be? She was truly scared to know the answer.

That morning, during breakfast, while Mrs. Dodgeson was already up in her office typing away on her book, and Mr. Dodgeson was pouring himself a bowl of cereal in the kitchen, Erin leaned closer to Becca over the table.

"Becca."

Her little sister shoveled another spoonful of chocolate and peanut butter cereal into her mouth. Lady Daisy, the stuffed elephant, sat on Becca's lap, her big purple eyes staring up at Erin from over the tabletop.

"Remember last night?" Erin asked, keeping her voice low while their father fixed his coffee. "When you woke up and heard me in the hallway?"

Becca moved her empty spoon to Lady Daisy's trunk in an attempt to feed the stuffed animal breakfast. "Yep," Becca said.

Erin swallowed. She didn't like how her sister wouldn't meet her gaze. "You asked if I was really ... *me*. Who did you think I was?"

Becca stopped. She put her spoon down and looked around. Her small face was serious and her lips were turned down in a frown. "Sometimes..." Her voice was so low that Erin had to lean closer over the table to hear. "Sometimes you make me call you Patty."

A shudder went through Erin. That name. She *knew* that name. She'd seen it before, scratched into the wall of the treehouse.

"Becca, what else did I say? What did I *do*?" Erin asked, breathless with fear. She knew she'd never told Becca to call her Patty—at least, not that she remembered. Could this have happened during the times she was sleepwalking? While she'd been drawing on the wall, while she'd gotten her mother's favorite mug from the kitchen? And if that were the case, then why? How? What did it mean?

Becca put her spoon into her bowl of cereal and mixed it around, still not meeting Erin's gaze. Almost like she was afraid to.

"Becca, you have to—"

Just then, their dad walked out of the kitchen and sat at the table. Not wanting to ask anything else while her father was there, Erin went back to her own cereal. As she ate, she tried to remember what else she'd seen in that treehouse. Was she *sure* that the name on the wall had been Patty? And if it was, it couldn't be just a simple coincidence. Was that name somehow tied to the blonde girl and her sleepwalking episodes?

Desperately, Erin hoped she was remembering the name wrong. Maybe it had been another *P* name, like Penny or Pamela? Though Erin didn't exactly want to, she knew it would bother her if she didn't find out for sure.

As she was summoning up her courage to return to the treehouse, her father surprised her by suggesting that the three of them go to the grocery store after breakfast.

"It's Saturday, and your mother could use some peace and quiet while working on her book," Mr. Dodgeson said, taking a sip of his coffee. "We've been so busy fixing up the house, we haven't really had time to drive into town yet."

"Yay!" Becca said, lifting her hands in the air so that Lady Daisy toppled off her lap.

"Sounds great," Erin said, a little more eager than usual.

Normally Erin would've disliked an outing with her family, but she was looking for an excuse to get out of going back to the treehouse. As much as she wanted to figure out what was going on, she wanted to avoid it as well.

Because what if what she feared . . . was real?

Their outing to town was busy. First, they went to the post office, then the hardware store (Mr. Dodgeson wanted to work on a few more do-it-yourself changes to the new house), and finally the grocery store. At the supermarket, Becca ran up and down the aisles and demanded every single kind of treat or snack. It was Erin's job to wrangle her younger sister while Mr. Dodgeson calmly went through their grocery list, comparing prices, finding things on sale, and then placing them in the cart.

By the time they got home, Erin was exhausted. (She did, however, have enough energy to stare down every house as they drove past, hoping to see Tara outside on her skateboard.) Becca had fallen asleep in the car and Mr. Dodgeson carried her up to her room while Erin got the groceries from the trunk.

As she was pulling the bags out, she noticed the boxes that she had packaged up and labeled last week. Apparently her father had put them in the car, but had yet to take them anywhere to get rid of them. One of the grocery bags, though, got caught on the edge of the box. She had to pull hard to yank it free and the box ended up falling on its side. When it did, she caught sight of the edge of a photo coming through the seam of the box.

A sudden and strange chill went through her. And without thinking, she grabbed the edge of the photo and slid it out from the box.

She almost dropped her grocery bags.

In the photo were two twin girls with blonde hair and bright smiles. One was holding a teddy bear, and the other's arm was slung around her sister's shoulders.

Of course Erin recognized the twins. Her worst fears suddenly had become a reality.

With trembling fingers, Erin folded up the old photo and tucked it into her back pocket and headed into the house.

Mrs. Dodgeson was in the kitchen, fixing herself a cup of tea while reading some printed pages from her new manuscript.

"Did you have fun at the grocery store?" Mrs. Dodgeson asked Erin as she put the milk and eggs in the fridge.

Erin just shrugged. She didn't trust herself to answer normally. Her mind was blank, and her heart was racing.

After the groceries were put away, Erin went upstairs to her room and sat at her desk and took out the photo to stare at it.

She was being haunted. She knew that for sure now. How else could she explain having seen one of the twins in the photo already? She saw this girl in her dreams and in the mirror. This photo had been tucked away among the previous owners' belongings, so there was only one possible conclusion for everything that was happening to her.

A ghost.

Erin shivered, placing the photo back on her desk. The horror of it had yet to fully sink in. Absently, she wondered which twin was Patty as she rested her head on her arms and spun the old globe lazily. Tracing the globe's surface with her fingertip, Erin watched the colors of the countries and the oceans blur together as her eyelids grew heavy and drooped . . .

Psst.

Erin jerked up in her desk chair, breathing hard.

The blonde girl stood over Erin, her curls hanging from her shoulders and her cheeks all rosy and warm. She wore the same pink dress as last time too.

"Wake up, sleepyhead," the blonde girl said, touching Erin's hand that still rested on her desk.

Erin wasn't fast enough to move away from the girl's touch. The moment the girl's icy fingers grazed Erin's skin, that strangely pleasant feeling took over once more. It was like Erin was dizzy, but happy, without a care in the world. When the blonde girl pulled Erin to her feet, Erin swayed on the spot a little, her head light but her heart pounding with furious anticipation—of what, she wasn't sure of yet.

"C'mon, let's get some hot chocolate," the girl said cheerily.

"Sure," Erin murmured as the blonde girl led her across the hall and down the stairs, their footsteps echoing loudly in the silence of the rest of the house. Even if she wanted to— and she didn't—she didn't have the strength to resist the girl. But a small voice in the back of her brain whispered, *This is wrong.*

As they neared the kitchen, Erin caught sight of something on the wall. Another photograph, like others she had seen other times.

I've seen this photo. I saw it today.

Within the old black-and-white photo were two girls who looked exactly the same. One of whom was standing right before her, holding her hand.

"Your sister," Erin rasped, before she could stop herself, "where is she?"

At that, the girl stopped and gave Erin a cold look. It was so cold that her blue eyes looked like ice and even her previously pink lips were tinged blue, like a corpse's. The girl smiled, her frozen lips drawing across her gleaming grin.

"What sister? I don't have a sister," was all the girl said.

Erin stared back, eyes wide, skin cold. *No, that's wrong. She's lying.* She had a sudden urge to yank out of the girl's grip and run, but she couldn't. Her body was too heavy, and her limbs were too weak.

In moments, they were in the kitchen. The blonde girl hummed a little tune as she took out a tub of cocoa mix and marshmallows and mugs.

"You get the hot water started," the girl instructed.

In the back of her mind, Erin wanted to refuse. But her hands moved anyway. She no longer seemed in control of her body. Even her thoughts were fragmented, like pieces of falling leaves that scattered to the wind.

Why is making hot chocolate bad? I should trust this girl. This was only a dream. I don't even want hot chocolate. But she said I love it.

Erin turned the dial on the gas stove and pretty blue flames sparked under the iron rungs. The blonde girl handed Erin the kettle and Erin placed the kettle on the iron ring, over the blue fire. The flames licked the bottom of the kettle, changing from a vibrant orange to an inky black.

That was odd. She'd never seen black flames before. Then they suddenly sparked and crackled loudly, and then leapt onto her shirt. With a gasp, Erin tried to put the black flames out by batting at her chest, but instead of disappearing, they latched on to her and spread. Like the black ooze, like the black spiders, this darkness wanted to devour her whole. It wrapped around her chest and jumped to her arms and up her throat.

"No! Stop!" Erin screamed. The black flames licked around her skin, burning her, but they weren't hot. It was a coldness so icy it burned, like touching a glacier. Like being trapped in ice.

Isn't this nice? You could be here forever, a voice as cold as the black flames whispered inside her chest.

"ERIN! STOP!"

The scream jolted Erin awake and out of her strange trance. Her head snapped to the side to find her mother standing in the kitchen doorway, looking absolutely horrified. But she had no idea why. Then, feeling a weird heat, Erin glanced down and stared in terror at the stack of papers—her mother's manuscript—in her grip, now on fire, thanks to them being held over the stove's flames. Before Erin could come to her senses, her mother raced over and grabbed the flaming papers and tossed them into the wet sink. The little bit of fire went out in a puff of smoke and steam as it was extinguished by the left-over soapy water from that morning's dishes.

Mrs. Dodgeson switched off the stove and turned to Erin.

Erin had never seen her mother like this. She looked upset beyond words. Her eyes were wide with fear, but her lips were turned down in anger and disappointment. Even her hands were shaking.

Before her mother could get out a single word, Erin broke down into sobs.

It was all too much. Her mother's terror and rage. The blonde girl appearing in her dreams. Making her do things against her will. This time she'd really crossed the line. Playing with fire was dangerous. Erin and her family could've been really hurt.

As she cried in her mother's arms, Erin knew one thing was certain: She couldn't deny what was happening a second longer.

Erin was being haunted and this ghost was *using* her body to do these awful things. It was why Becca had said Erin had made her call her Patty. Because Erin wasn't Erin when she was doing these things. She was somehow the ghost—*Patty*.

But how could Erin stop the ghost? And could she tell her parents? Would her parents believe her, or would the truth make everything worse?

Once Erin had finally stopped sobbing, her mother and father sat with her in her room. Her mother was on the bed next to her, rubbing circles on her back, while her father leaned against the door, watching her with sad, concerned eyes.

"Erin, sweetie, what happened?" her mother said softly. Her voice sounded pained. And why wouldn't it be? Erin's behavior wasn't making any sense. And even a professional child therapist—like her mother—could be lost on how to handle her own child's problems.

Erin couldn't answer. She didn't know what to say that didn't sound completely impossible. That didn't sound like she was making things up for attention.

"You know you can tell us anything," her father tried.

But could she? Erin really considered telling her parents

about the ghost and about the sleepwalking episodes. But she just couldn't bring herself to form the words. She didn't want to see their disappointment, confusion, even *pity* on their faces as they struggled to understand what Erin was going through.

Because they can't, Erin thought, twisting her fingers in her lap. *They've never been haunted. How could they know what I'm going through? Why would they ever believe me?*

Her mother sighed. "Erin, we're not leaving here until we get *some* explanation."

Erin swallowed down another lump in her throat. "I'd turned on the stove to make some mac and cheese because I was hungry. I thought I could do it by myself, but then your papers were by the stove and they caught fire and I just froze. I'm sorry."

There was a long silence in her room after the lie. And she wasn't sure if her parents would really believe her, but in the end, they did. Probably because they wanted to. Because they couldn't think of any other reason why Erin would do such a thing.

After her parents left her room, Erin felt determination harden in her stomach. She *had* to go to the treehouse. It seemed to be where it all had started. It was where the ghost's name, *Patty*, was carved into the wall. Maybe Erin could talk to the ghost and find out what her unfinished business was. Wasn't that how ghost stories usually worked? Their spirits remained behind because something important to them kept them from being able to move on. Maybe the ghost was looking for something. Like an old doll or a diary, and Erin just needed to help her find it so she could rest in peace.

It was worth a try.

It was worth anything to stop all these terrible things from happening. To stop her parents from thinking she was either turning into a horrible, destructive person, or that she was a deeply troubled kid. Which, considering she was being haunted by a ghost, wasn't that far from the truth.

10

That night, Erin didn't bother trying to go to sleep. She went through the motions of getting ready for bed, like washing her face and brushing her teeth and putting on her pajamas. But then she just lay there, wide awake, waiting to make sure her parents and little sister were asleep before she hurried downstairs.

When she'd slipped on her shoes and stepped out onto the porch, she instantly wanted to turn around and go back inside. The outside world was dark. Very dark. Erin had forgotten what it was like to be out in the country without streetlights and all of the city lights from storefronts, apartment buildings, and public transportation. Out here, it was just the moon and the stars, *if* they were out.

Unfortunately, it was a cloudy night and Mr. Dodgeson had turned off the porch light. Erin could barely see her hand in front of her face, let alone the planks up to the treehouse. It would've been easy to use the darkness as an excuse not to go up to the treehouse, but Erin couldn't take even another day of this. What was next after turning on the stove? She couldn't even fathom anything worse, but that didn't mean the ghost—Patty—couldn't.

As Erin felt her way down the porch steps, her foot nudged a crate of tools her father had laid out from their trip to the hardware store earlier that day. Vaguely, Erin remembered her father sticking a flashlight in the box of tools.

"Come on, come on . . ." Erin muttered as she crouched down and rummaged around inside the toolbox. She moved aside a hammer, screwdriver, and then let out a sigh of relief when she felt the cool metal of a flashlight. She flicked it on and the gold beam stretched across the grass of the backyard.

It was somehow . . . creepier. The one beam of light made the rest of the backyard darker. The edges of the darkness pressed in on Erin, the inky blackness threatening to swallow her whole if the flashlight went out. It reminded her of moments from her nightmares, where the darkness spread over her and devoured her. She prayed the flashlight had enough battery life.

With a hard swallow, Erin began making her way across the grass toward the giant oak tree. Unlike a few days ago, where it had been rainy and muddy, the dry grass crunched under her feet. Crickets chirped loudly, and what sounded like an army of frogs bellowed at the top of their lungs. Wind blew through the leaves, creating a rustling sound. Altogether, the sounds were actually soothing. It comforted Erin to know that it wasn't just empty darkness beyond the beams of her flashlight. There was an entire world out there.

When the light fell upon the roots of the old tree, Erin blew out a breath. She was almost there. Strangely, she didn't know how to feel. Did she *want* to encounter the ghost? Or did she want this to be a colossal waste of time?

No. I have to figure this out myself, Erin thought as she moved forward and tucked the flashlight under her chin. She would need both hands to climb the wooden planks nailed on the tree. Erin gritted her teeth, and, as she climbed, the summer-night breeze seemed to get colder. It made her shiver and cling to the planks of wood with trembling chilly fingers. How had a summer night grown so cold, so fast?

Also, how had it gotten so quiet?

Not even a minute ago, the backyard had been full of noises. A chorus of nocturnal creatures, singing their hearts out, had all gone completely silent. Like someone had shut a soundproof door behind Erin.

Shadows danced around her legs from the flashlight's beam bobbing up and down under her chin. Low-hanging branches and leaves created a sort of canopy of darkness over her and she tried to climb faster.

Finally she reached the last plank and her hair brushed the top of the wood. Carefully Erin held on with one hand while she took her flashlight in the other and pointed the beam up into the treehouse.

The ghost was right above Erin, waiting in the doorframe.

Her blonde curls hung and framed her white face, while the rest of her body was translucent in the flashlight's beam. But that wasn't even the scariest part. Her eyes were white and milky without any pupils, the skin on her face and hands was pulled tautly across her bones, and her lips were that same icy-blue tint from the dream.

Erin was too frightened to even move. She wasn't even sure how she managed to stay holding on to the plank nailed to the tree. Something kept her there. Like a force she couldn't describe or explain.

"Paula," the ghost rasped. The air that wheezed through the ghost's lungs rattled and whistled something terrible. Her corpse-like hand shot out and grabbed Erin by the wrist. Erin dropped the flashlight and screamed. Just like in her nightmares, darkness enveloped Erin. But this time she could see a pair of milky-white eyes staring down, unblinking. Then, cold like Erin had never experienced before started from her wrist and spread through her body like ice. It froze her blood. Just when Erin didn't think she'd be able to withstand another second, a blast of wind came whooshing out of the treehouse and hit Erin with full force.

Erin couldn't hold on. She fell.

The fall took less than a second, and yet it seemed to take an hour too. That terrible cold reached her heart, and then traveled up her neck. And as she hit the grass, she felt a twist in her wrist, a searing, hot pain, and then . . .

She felt nothing at all.

11

Erin opened her eyes to branches and leaves and dots of bright sunlight shining through. It was such a beautiful scene that Erin felt peaceful as she lay there on the grass, looking up. But as minutes ticked by, she started to question how she got there. Why was she just lying on the grass under the oak tree in the middle of the day? Had she fallen asleep again? Had she...

Her gaze found the treehouse then, and slowly the memory of last night trickled back to her.

She'd fallen from the treehouse because of the ghost. Patty had been there, maybe waiting for her. It had been the single most terrifying moment of Erin's life. One second the treehouse had been empty, and the next, the ghost was there in the bright beam of the flashlight.

At the thought of the flashlight, Erin remembered she had dropped it. Before she went back inside and snuck up to her bedroom so her parents wouldn't discover she spent the night outside, she'd better search for her dad's flashlight.

Erin sat up and gingerly got to her feet, surprised to find that she wasn't hurt. Not even a bump on the head. Erin had fallen a fair distance, so it seemed strange that she didn't even feel any bruises.

"Patty? You okay?"

Erin jumped at the voice and twisted around, her heels digging into the grass.

Seeing the girl before her, Erin gasped. It was the ghost. But this time, she looked *alive*. Rosy cheeks and bright blue eyes. But . . . wait. Why was the ghost calling Erin Patty? Wasn't *she* Patty?

That's when Erin noticed the small differences. Unlike Patty's curls and waves, this girl's hair was silky straight. She also looked a bit tanner and had freckles, like she got to spend more time out in the sun. Instead of a pink dress, she wore a blue dress with pearl-snap buttons down the middle.

The photograph came back to Erin suddenly and that's when

she remembered—twins. This girl was Patty's twin. This girl was "P."

Erin couldn't help but wonder, *Is she a ghost too?*

"Did you have another attack, Pat?" the girl called P asked, bending down next to Erin and placing a warm hand on Erin's cool, clammy forehead.

Erin jerked away, not wanting to be touched by the strange girl. Especially not one who was potentially dead. "A-attack?"

Patty's twin frowned, giving Erin a strange look. "You're not coughing." Then she glanced up, behind Erin, and her frown deepened. "You didn't try climbing up to the treehouse, did you? Papa said he was going to nail down the planks to the tree next weekend so we could have a ladder."

Nothing this girl was saying made any sense. Coughing? Attacks? *Papa?* Why was she talking to Erin like Erin was Patty? And while it was a small thing compared to everything else, Erin knew the oak tree *already* had planks on the trunk because she had just used them last night.

Erin turned around, afraid to look but knowing she had to. Sure enough, the planks on the tree were gone. But they had *just* been there last night. How was this possible?

The girl touched Erin's shoulder as she asked, "How far did you fall, Patty? Should I go get Mama?"

Her touch felt *real.* Warm and solid. Not like that of a ghost's. Erin knocked her hand away, her heart pounding in her chest. "I'm *not* Patty."

How was this all possible? How were the planks gone? How was this twin alive when Patty was dead? And probably had been, for a long time now? Unless . . . was she caught in another strange dream? Could that be what this was? A dream . . . that belonged to the ghost?

Except before, she'd never known she was in a dream. This was different than those other times. This felt more real. More . . . permanent.

Erin tried not to panic. Instead, she looked on the bright side. This could be her opportunity to find out about the ghost and her past. Maybe this was Patty's unfinished business!

The twin looked hurt as she moved her hand away. "Um, what do you mean you're not Patty?" She tucked a curtain of long gold hair behind her ear, her light brows furrowing. Then her blue eyes lit up with excitement. "Oh, is this a game? Are we playing cops and robbers? Aces! I'll be the fuzz. Here, you can take Teddy." She thrust a stuffed bear into Erin's arms. "He can be your hostage."

The girl pretended to draw an invisible gun. "In the name of the law, grab the air or I'll fill ya with lead!"

Erin simply held the teddy bear, lost for words. This girl talked *weird*. The fuzz? Grab the air? Fill with lead? Talking to Patty's twin may be more difficult than Erin imagined. How could she figure out Patty's unfinished business when she could hardly understand half of what this girl said?

Before she could respond, a woman's voice yelled across the backyard.

"Paula! Come help me fold laundry."

Erin's breath caught in her chest. *Paula.*

"No playing outside, it's much too hot today. Let your sister rest!"

Erin's gaze followed the sound of the voice until it landed on a figure under the porch awning. The woman stood on the steps holding a basket of freshly washed clothes. She wore a simple floral dress and her hair was long and blonde as well. But her features were hard to make out in the awning's shadows.

The twin with the straight blonde hair—Paula—turned

around and hollered back. "I'm coming, Mama!" Then she turned back to Erin and whispered, "We'll play in our room later."

Paula ran toward the porch and joined her mother. She took the other basket of laundry from the steps, and together, they went into the house.

For a moment, Erin could do nothing but stand there and stare after them in shock. *Paula.* She knew that name too. It was the name the ghost had whispered. Once in the hallway next to her ear, and then once more right before she grabbed Erin's wrist last night in the treehouse.

Did Patty's unfinished business have something to do with her sister, Paula?

"Wait!" Erin called, dropping the teddy bear. She tried to run, but after only a few steps a sudden pain in her chest made her trip. "W-wait up!" she choked. Her lungs felt shriveled and dry as she tried to breathe through the pain that squeezed her ribs.

Why was she feeling this way? Her skin felt achy and feverish. Was she sick?

Erin walked across the backyard, each step more shaky than the last. Sweat rolled down her jaw and her breath came out in short, shallow pants. It wasn't until Erin reached the house that she looked up and noticed her reflection in one of the windows.

She froze and stared.

What she saw in the glass was not her short brown hair, rounded face, and brown eyes. It was Patty's face. The ghost. Curly blonde hair that hung past her shoulders, blue eyes, and pale skin with sunken cheeks.

Erin couldn't look away as horror crawled over her skin like a spider. It couldn't—*shouldn't*—be possible. It was like that time in the bathroom mirror, except now Erin knew with absolute certainty that she really was in Patty's body. With shaking hands, Erin pulled at her hair and found the strands between her fingers to be long, curly, and blonde.

She let out a soft whimper as her breath came out in panicked dry sobs. A voice whispered inside her head, the words hauntingly familiar.

Isn't this nice? You could be here forever.

This couldn't be real. She couldn't stay like this. She couldn't be Patty, forever, in this dream world. And if this was really a dream, she needed to wake up.

Wake up! Wake up!

Behind her, she felt someone's fingers rake through her hair. Erin squealed and batted the hand away from her, but she felt nothing except air. Only . . . when she looked up into the window, she found another Patty behind her. The ghost of Patty—with white, milky eyes, blue lips, and skin stretched tight across the bones of her dead face.

Erin squeezed her eyes shut and screamed.

12

Erin awoke with a gasp, her scream still echoing in her head and vibrating in her chest. Her heart was galloping like a race-horse, but the moment her vision focused on the furniture of her room, a warm blanket of relief fell on her trembling shoulders.

She was back home. In her room. With her desk, her books, her *National Geographic* posters.

Just to make sure though, she reached up and touched her hair. It was back to being short and brown. She threaded it through her fingers, and the continual motion gave her comfort. She was back in her own body, and she was touching her own hair. Back to being Erin. No ghost. No blonde curls.

She was so relieved that it took her much too long to realize that there was a neon-pink brace on her left wrist.

Erin rotated her arm in shock. A brace? Why was she wearing a brace? How had she gotten it? Vaguely, she remembered that when she fell from the treehouse last night she'd felt something snap in her wrist and then a pinch of concentrated pain had quickly followed. But when had she gone to the hospital to get a brace? Had it happened during the night while Erin had been trapped in the ghost's dream? But why didn't she remember it? Surely her parents would've noticed that Erin had been asleep the whole time, or sleepwalking, at the very least.

Knowing her parents had to have all the answers, Erin slipped out of bed and headed downstairs. She found her family already seated at the kitchen table eating a breakfast of toast and eggs.

"Good morning, Erin," Mrs. Dodgeson said with a smile, looking up from reading something off her tablet. "Did you sleep well?"

Erin blinked. The last time she had broken a bone had been because she'd landed wrong on her ankle while jumping for a basket during gym class. For nearly five days her mother had fussed over her ankle, asking if it hurt, making sure she was using her crutches correctly, et cetera. It seemed strange that the day after she'd broken her wrist, her mother wouldn't ask about it at all.

If it hadn't been for the weight, and the itchy, hot feeling of the brace, Erin would have wondered if she was just imagining it on her arm. Because her parents didn't look bothered by it at all.

"Um." Erin swallowed. "How bad was the break?"

Erin figured that was a safe enough question. Clearly her parents didn't seem particularly worried about the injury, so she didn't want to alarm them in admitting she had no memory of the hospital visit whatsoever.

Mr. and Mrs. Dodgeson both looked up from their plates, giving Erin a strange look. Then they exchanged glances at each other, then turned back to Erin. "You mean your ... wrist?" her mother asked.

"Well, yeah," Erin said hesitantly.

"It's not a break, sweetie. You just sprained it. Should be fine in a couple weeks. The doctor repeated it several times," Mr. Dodgeson said, taking a sip of his coffee. "Why? Is it bothering you?"

No, it wasn't. In fact, it didn't hurt at all. Which was also a little strange. If the sprain had happened just last night, why didn't it hurt more?

"Um, no. Did I take pain medicine?" Erin asked.

Again, her parents gave her a weird look. Mrs. Dodgeson shook her head. "You haven't taken medicine in three days, when you first sprained it."

Erin almost fell over, her knees buckling in shock.

Three . . . *days*?

Panic rose inside her like a tidal wave, threatening to pull Erin under and drown her. But before it could, she fought it back with a strong dose of complete denial.

That couldn't be right. She couldn't be missing *three whole days*. There had to be some mistake. Or maybe . . . maybe she was dreaming again. There was just no way it was possible. That would mean that—

No. No. *No.* This had to be a mistake. Or a joke. Maybe her parents were playing a prank on her. If they were, it was mean and *not* funny.

"That's not funny," Erin said loudly.

Mrs. Dodgeson's frown deepened. "What's not funny?"

"I fell out of the treehouse *last* night," Erin stated, before she could take it back. "Not three nights ago."

Her father sighed, his gaze full of disappointment, while her mother gave her a harsh look. "I swear, Erin," Mrs. Dodgeson said, her tone bordering on angry. "What has been up with you recently? You've been odd the last few days, but at least all of the incidents stopped. The worst is that you've just been acting like you forgot where everything is. But this is a step too far. I just don't know what you're going to come up with next."

Erin's heart pounded in her eardrums and her mother's voice faded into white noise. She couldn't hear or focus on anything else. What her mother was describing . . . it made it sound like Erin had been walking and talking for three whole days, but had it really been *her*? Or someone else acting like her?

Afraid her face revealed the panic she felt, Erin turned on her heel and raced upstairs.

"Erin?" her mom called after her. "We're not done here!"

"I'll be right back!" Erin yelled, though her voice sounded strangled and high-pitched. Her feet carried her into her bedroom, where she snatched her cell phone off her bedside table.

Strangely, it had dust on it, like it hadn't been touched in a couple days. Sure, it wasn't like Erin used her cell phone often. Her parents restricted her usage of it to phone games and texting. She didn't have social media yet, nor was she allowed to use the Internet on it because of "data usage," as her dad explained. Even so, she picked it up occasionally to text her friends back in Chicago and play some of her favorite games before she went to bed.

But if Erin hadn't been *Erin*, she guessed it made sense why it looked like she hadn't touched it in days.

Quickly, she unlocked the screen and stared in horror at the date: Wed, June 25, 8:16 a.m.

It had been Saturday night when Erin had visited the treehouse. Instead of Sunday, it was Wednesday. Three whole days later. Three whole days that Erin couldn't remember.

"This can't be real, this can't be real," Erin muttered to herself as she stared at her phone screen for several long minutes, willing the date and time to change back. Back to Saturday, even, where she could've stopped herself from ever returning to that treehouse.

What was she supposed to do now? Should she tell her

parents that she honestly didn't remember the last few days? And that the Erin they *thought* they had been living with wasn't the *real* Erin but—

She shook her head fiercely, trying to shake the horrible thought out of her brain. Just because she didn't remember the last three days didn't mean that the ghost had actually taken over her body and acted as her. Maybe it was the result of her fall. Maybe it was a side effect of a head injury where she couldn't remember chunks of time.

That was possible. That seemed logical, even. She bet her parents would understand and accept that.

Still, she was desperate to find out what she'd missed. What had happened in her life for three days that she didn't know about?

Luckily there was a way to find out. Her mother, being a successful child therapist, kept an active Instagram account, posting inspirational stories, parenting tips, and chronicling her own family events.

Even though Erin wasn't yet allowed to use social media, she knew how it worked and how to find her mother's account. Her mother had even let Erin search through the social media platform looking at animal videos and scenic photos from around the world.

Holding her breath, Erin found her mother's most recent post, which was from three days ago. It was a group of photos of the Dodgeson family at a local park. They were all standing by the park sign, making goofy faces and pointing at it. The sign read PEMBLEBROOK PARK. In the photo, Mrs. Dodgeson stood behind Erin, who was holding up her new neon-pink brace while Mr. Dodgeson had Becca on his shoulders. The next photo was of them all eating ice cream. They looked happy, and Erin in the picture was laughing, with a dollop of strawberry ice cream on her nose.

"You've got to be *kidding* me."

Erin had trouble believing what she was seeing. How *weird* it was to look at photos of herself from just a couple days ago with no memory of it! Not to mention, Erin hated strawberry ice cream—she always went for chocolate instead.

She scrolled through the last three photos. The third was of Erin and Mr. Dodgeson attempting to fly a kite, the fourth was of Mrs. Dodgeson and Becca on the swings, and the fifth was of Erin and—Erin couldn't believe it. *Tara!*

The girl with the skateboard from the neighborhood was standing in the park's soccer field, a net and other kids running and kicking a ball in the background. The photo was clearly a candid shot. Erin had been watching the kids play soccer while Tara had picked up a ball by the fence post. Erin wondered if Tara had talked to her, and if she did, had she mentioned their first meeting? At least now she knew where she could perhaps find Tara to ask her more about the rumors surrounding the treehouse that Erin had brushed off a couple of weeks ago.

With that hope, Erin turned her attention to the caption of the social media post that her mother had written:

Had a blast with the fam at the park today! And yes, before any of you ask, Erin sprained her wrist. By falling out of a tree, of all things! No matter how much you want to protect your kids, accidents are bound to happen. But our girl is brave and strong! Not a single tear when we took her to the hospital this morning. We rewarded her by visiting our new town's city park and it was a much-needed break after the move and all the unpacking. Erin also met some local kids and could be interested in soccer camp this summer! There are still open slots so we'll see after her wrist heals. From our family to yours. #PemblebrookPark #parenting #DodgesonFamilyOuting

Erin sat back in the computer chair and drew her knees up to her chest, trying hard not to cry. She was too overwhelmed by everything. The ghost. Losing her memory. And now *this*. It was difficult to explain in words, but seeing these pictures and reading this post made Erin feel incredibly lonely and empty inside.

Normally Erin would hate family outings like this. She liked going off and doing her own thing. Exploring and being independent, especially lately because of her growing annoyance with having to take care of Becca all the time. But with all the recent incidents, her parents had grown frustrated with, angry at, and disappointed in Erin. In many ways, Erin felt like she was losing her mom and dad. At the very least, she was losing their trust.

She didn't want to tell them anything that would make that trust disappear entirely. So that meant she couldn't tell them about the lost days, *or* the ghost. She had to face Patty alone, whenever she showed up again.

13

"You want to do what?" Mrs. Dodgeson finally looked away from her computer screen to squint at Erin suspiciously through her thick-framed glasses.

"Take Becca to the park," Erin repeated.

It was only a single day after waking up and discovering she was missing three entire calendar days. No ghost-related incidents had happened since then, but Erin was on edge. Every little sound, every little weird feeling had her checking over her shoulder or wanting to hide under the covers. Her desire to return to Pemblebrook Park had to do with several factors. One, she just wanted to escape this house where the ghost showed up in mirrors and took control of her when she napped. Two, she was jealous that this "other Erin" had been able to visit the park and she had no recollection of it whatsoever. Three, maybe actually visiting it could jog some memory of her time there. And four, most importantly, she hoped to run into Tara and *finally* get some answers.

"Your wrist is still sprained, honey. You wouldn't really be able to play," Mrs. Dodgeson said, starting to turn her chair back to the computer screen.

"I wasn't able to play on Sunday and we still went," Erin pointed out. "And I can just watch Becca while she's on the playground."

Mrs. Dodgeson paused her typing and gave Erin a side-eyed look. It was odd for Erin to *offer* to watch Becca. Her parents knew she viewed it more as a chore—one that Erin did most of the time without complaint, but a chore nonetheless.

"Well..." her mother said slowly. "The library is across the street from the park and I could use a change of scenery in writing this chapter. I guess it's all right, then, if you're really fine with it."

Erin nodded eagerly, relief spreading through her.

"Go get Becca ready, then," Erin's mother said as she started packing up her laptop bag.

Not needing to be told twice, Erin hurried into Becca's room to find her little sister on her bed, surrounded by her stuffed animals and seven crayons deep into a princess coloring book.

"Becca, do you want to go to the park?" Erin asked as she went to her sister's closet to grab her shoes.

Becca dropped her crayons and her face lit up with a grin. "Yeah! Can Mr. Fuzzy Hooves come?"

Any other time, Erin would've tried to talk her little sister out of bringing along her stuffed giraffe, but she nodded and grabbed Becca's sparkly pink backpack and tucked Mr. Fuzzy Hooves inside.

Ten minutes later, they were ready and in the car. Mrs. Dodgeson pulled out of the driveway and headed down the long road. Erin watched the other houses pass by, and once again looked for Tara. But she didn't see the girl, so she *hoped* she'd be at the park.

For the hundredth time, she wondered what rumor it was that Tara knew about that treehouse. Would the story behind it help Erin figure out how the ghost could finally move on and rest, spiritually?

Those thoughts were still bouncing around in Erin's mind when her mother dropped her and Becca off at Pemblebrook

Park. Erin recognized the park and the scenery from her mother's social media post. It was a really big park with three soccer fields, two tennis courts, a playground, walking trails, several picnic tables, a set of restrooms, and Erin even spotted an ice cream stand across the way.

"I'll pick you up at three thirty so be wary of time," her mother said, tapping her watch. "And use your phone if you need me."

Erin nodded while Becca jumped up and down next to her yelling, "Swings! Swings! Swings!"

As Mrs. Dodgeson pulled away from the curb's entrance to the park, Erin checked the time on her cell phone. Since it was one thirty now, that meant they had two hours to play at the park. It wasn't as long as Erin would've liked, but she definitely wasn't going to complain.

"Swings! Swings! Swings!" Becca kept yelling at the top of her lungs and tugged on Erin's shirt.

Then again . . . maybe two hours with her little sister was *too much* time.

"Okay, okay," Erin snapped, grabbing Becca's hand. The little girl bounded toward the playground, half skipping and tugging Erin's good arm. As soon as they reached the swings, Becca let go, dropped her pink backpack, and hopped onto the first one.

"Push me, Erin! Push me!"

Erin grimaced. It was going to be harder to push with an injured wrist, but not impossible. "I will if you stop wiggling," she said.

Becca stopped scooching around in the swing and remained still. With her right hand, Erin gave Becca a solid push and up into the air she went.

"Wheeee!" Becca screamed to the sky as she began to swing her legs back and forth to help gain momentum. Erin kept pushing her, mostly so Becca wouldn't get upset if she stopped.

They played on the swings for a good while before Becca turned to Erin and gave her a large grin. "I'm glad you're able to finally go to the park too, Erin."

At her sister's words, a sort of chill trickled down Erin's spine. With her good hand, she grabbed the chain of the swing and stopped it. "What do you mean by *finally*, Becca? We . . . we all came here together on Sunday, right?"

Becca's smile vanished. She looked down at her knees and

dug her feet into the woodchips of the playground. "Nothing," she said, her voice all quiet and sad.

Erin squatted down next to Becca, her heartbeat starting to race. "Becks, you can tell me. You know it wasn't me on Sunday, don't you?"

Her little sister refused to meet her eyes. Becca stared at the ground instead, and then cried out suddenly, "Look! Erin! Soccer!" She leapt from the swing and raced toward the soccer fields where a group of kids were running and kicking a ball around.

"Becca! Wait!" Erin cried. With an aggravated sigh, Erin snatched up Becca's backpack and hurried after the five-year-old.

Thankfully Becca had enough sense to not run straight into the soccer fields where the older kids were kicking the ball around with all their strength. Erin joined Becca at the sidelines, taking her hand to make sure she didn't run off again.

As they watched the kids play, Erin almost shouted and jumped in triumph, and relief. One of the players was familiar—brown skin, long braids tied up, a blue soccer jersey. It was Tara.

She's really here!

Surprisingly, Becca recognized her too because she yelled out, "Tara! HI!"

Tara looked over in confusion as she was running down the field. When her gaze fell on Becca and Erin, she waved back.

Uh-oh. Immediately, Erin started worrying. If Becca had talked to Tara, then it was highly possible that Tara had tried to talk to Erin on Sunday. But if Erin wasn't really Erin ... what had she said?

The kids on the field played for a bit longer before someone on Tara's team scored a goal and a whistle blew. They all erupted in cheers and claps on the back. Becca proceeded to jump up and down, waving, and nearly yanking Erin's good arm out of its socket.

"Tara! Tara! Hi!"

Tara jogged over. She was sweaty and stained with grass, but Erin thought she looked really cool because of it.

"Hi, Becca!" Tara said, raising her hand, and Becca met it with a high five. She glanced at Erin, but the look was brief and unreadable.

"Hey ..." Erin said, not exactly sure what else to say.

"Are you guys back at the park today? Where's your mom and dad?" Tara asked, once again addressing Becca.

"It's just me and Erin today. This is my *real* sister, Erin," Becca said, squeezing Erin's hand and smiling happily.

Tara tilted her head in confusion at Becca's words and Erin swallowed uncomfortably. "Um, she just means I wasn't exactly myself on Sunday."

"Oh. Is that why you were a little rude?" Tara asked bluntly.

Again, Erin was at a loss for words. It was obvious that the "other Erin" hadn't exactly been friendly to Tara and now *she*, the *real* Erin, was paying for it. It was unfair that Erin had to apologize for behavior that wasn't hers, but . . .

She liked Tara. Not only was she a good athlete, but she seemed honest and straightforward, and Erin liked that in a friend. Not someone who would talk about her behind her back. Plus, Erin was desperate for new friends here.

"Uh . . . I mean, yeah, sorry about that. I'd hurt my wrist the night before and I guess I was a little grumpy," Erin said awkwardly.

"You acted like you had no idea who I was," Tara said, a trace of hurt in her voice.

Erin winced. *Oh no.*

"That . . . I mean . . ."

"Did you score any goals, Tara?" Becca piped in.

Tara looked away from Erin to smile down at Becca. "Not today, but I passed the ball to a friend so she could make the goal."

"Can I play?" Becca asked.

"Becca—" Erin began, thinking that Tara had to leave, or maybe even had better things to do than play soccer with a five-year-old.

"Sure," Tara said cheerfully, and she gestured for the two sisters to follow her across the field. "Official practice is over, so we can kick the ball around a bit." Tara took a ball from a nearby sports bag and tossed it on the grass. It rolled toward Becca and Becca gave it one solid kick. To Erin's surprise, it went a pretty decent distance. Immediately, Becca took off toward the ball, kicking it clumsily down the field as Erin and Tara watched.

"So how'd you hurt it?" Tara asked.

Erin glanced down at her wrist and swallowed thickly.

"I fell out of the treehouse," Erin muttered. She was almost ashamed to admit it. Tara had told her to stay away from it, and here she was with her wrist injured because of it.

Tara tore her gaze away from Becca kicking her ball across the field and looked at Erin with wide eyes. She blew out a breath and shook her head, her ponytail of braids swishing back and forth. "I *told* you not to go in it."

"But you didn't tell me why," Erin shot back.

"Yeah, well . . . you wouldn't have believed me anyway," Tara grumbled as she snatched up her water bottle and tipped it into her mouth.

Of course she was right. Erin had dismissed her immediately when they first met, and had even made up an excuse to leave to avoid hearing any dumb rumors.

Well. She was ready to hear them now.

"I'll believe you now. I promise," Erin said.

Tara didn't look up. Just shrugged and proceeded to clean off her soccer cleats with a towel. "Yeah, right."

Erin's hands curled into fists. She kinda knew she deserved this, especially when she had basically blown Tara off not once, but twice. But she couldn't not hear about the rumor. She had to get Tara to believe her.

"I've seen her, you know."

Tara froze in wiping down her cleats and slowly turned her head to look at Erin with wide eyes.

Knowing Erin had Tara's interest now, she dug into her back pocket and pulled out the old photo that she'd kept in one of her desk drawers since the day she'd found it. Erin lowered her voice as she handed the photo to Tara, but said slowly and clearly, "I've seen the *ghost*. I've seen *her*." Erin tapped the face of Patty in the photo.

Lips parted in shock, Tara took the photo. "No . . . way . . ."

At that moment, Becca came running back with the soccer ball. She was covered in flecks of grass and green stains but she looked happy. "Did you see, Erin? Did you see? I kicked it into the goal!"

"Good job," Erin said, forcing a smile while quickly taking the photo back and stuffing it into her pocket.

Annoyance pricked at her. What terrible timing. They couldn't talk about ghosts in front of Becca. It would either scare her and give her nightmares or Becca would tattle to their parents about it. And while Erin suspected that Becca knew *something* was different about the treehouse—about Erin's missing memories and the fact that she wasn't always herself—Becca obviously never wanted to talk about it. It was as if she was afraid to admit that it was all real.

Which, Erin had to admit, had been her first instinct too. They were definitely sisters, and thought alike.

Tara took her soccer ball back from Becca and looked to Erin. Her brows were furrowed, and she was biting her bottom lip. The way she was acting made it clear that she very much wanted to hear more about the ghost.

"I have to go, but . . . do you have a cell?" Tara asked.

Fighting back a large sigh of relief, Erin fumbled for her phone and pulled it out. "Yeah, what's your number?"

Tara gave it to her and then Erin texted her so Tara would have hers as well. "I'll text you," Tara said, giving Erin a meaningful look as she shouldered her sports bag.

After Tara left, Erin and Becca headed back to the playground, and some of the fear in Erin's chest lessened slightly. She was one step closer to figuring out the mystery behind Patty and the haunted treehouse.

14

The rest of the day, Erin kept an eye on her phone. She wanted Tara to text so badly. Now that she was back home, where any moment it felt like Patty could come back in some way— through her dreams or through another mirror—Erin was even more desperate to learn about the ghostly rumors surrounding the treehouse.

She even went so far as to bring her phone to dinner and check for texts under the table. Luckily her parents didn't notice because they were too busy talking about how Becca could take soccer lessons along with Erin.

Finally, after doing the dishes and before she was about to get ready for bed, Erin's phone pinged with a new message. She nearly dropped it in her excitement. Holding her breath, she opened up her messages.

TARA: So have you really seen the ghost?

Erin stared at the message, wondering how to respond. She didn't want to sound overeager or enthusiastic, because then it wouldn't feel genuine. She needed Tara to believe her. The last thing she wanted was for Tara to think Erin was making things up to be friends.

Tongue between her teeth, Erin typed out:

ERIN: I honestly wasn't sure what I saw at first. But I've seen a girl with blonde curly hair once in the treehouse. And another time in a mirror. It was really creepy.

Again, this was nothing but the truth. However, she definitely didn't want to tell Tara about Patty visiting her dreams—or making her do things. That was *too* weird to admit that. Yet.

TARA: No. Way. Are you for REAL?!

Erin blew out a breath. At least Tara wasn't claiming that she was making this up. Quickly she typed out:

ERIN: I swear! I didn't even believe in ghosts. Until I moved here.

TARA: Wow. I grew up hearing about the treehouse, but I've never actually SEEN Patty.

A chill went down Erin's spine. *Patty.*

Erin had never felt so relieved and so spooked at the same time. At least now she knew this wasn't all in her head. She really was being haunted. And apparently Pemblebrook even knew the ghost's name and had rumors about her.

TARA: We should talk about this in person. When can you meet up?

Erin couldn't type back fast enough.

ERIN: I'll ask my parents tomorrow.

A tapping noise woke Erin up. She blinked through the darkness of her room, chasing sleep from the corners of her mind as the rapping and scratching grew louder.

Irritated, Erin turned onto her side and slammed the pillow over her head. It was the branches hitting the window again. They had done this a few nights before, but she'd always managed to fall asleep regardless. Now, though, they seemed intent on keeping her up.

The tree branches scraped across the glass, sounding more like human fingernails—or something even sharper. If Erin believed in monsters, then she would've said it sounded a bit like claws, but she knew that was impossible.

146

As impossible as ghosts? a little voice inside her head taunted.

Erin gritted her teeth and squeezed her eyes shut, just wanting to go back to her dreamless, peaceful sleep.

Two seconds later, all of the sounds stopped, and Erin breathed a relieved sigh. The summer-night wind must have died down. Just as she was on the cusp of sleep, Erin felt her covers slip from around her shoulders to her chest.

Like someone was pulling them down.

Goose bumps crawling across her skin, Erin peeked from under her pillow and watched as the covers moved on their own. They slipped down her pajamas, all the way to her hips. With a gasp, Erin jerked upright and grabbed the covers, tugging them all the way up to her chin. In that moment, she swore someone was pulling the covers on the opposite side. She actually had to use her muscles to yank the covers away from the invisible grip.

Panting, Erin slipped back down into her bed and pulled the sheets over her head.

"Go away," Erin whispered under her breath. "Please, ple—"

She let out a sharp cry as an icy grip tightened around her ankle and gave a brutal tug. It felt like a real hand on her skin—but a hand harboring the coldness of death. The pull was so strong and so sudden that Erin slid off the bed. Her feet hit the floor first, and then her backside, the covers still over her head.

She threw the sheets away from her shoulders and clumsily got to her feet, stumbling over to her door. She was seconds away from bolting into the hallway when she heard a voice.

Paula.

Erin froze at the sound of the cold, raspy words. It sounded like the person wasn't just in the room with her, but right beside her.

Real, awful *terror* had Erin physically shaking. Shaking so hard her knees were knocking together. But she had to look— she had to *face* this ghost. If Patty was here in the room with her, then Erin had to figure out what she wanted. So she could go away for good.

Slowly Erin turned to look over her shoulder. For better or for worse, the room itself was empty. Patty's spirit still seemed to be invisible when *not* inside Erin's dreams, or the treehouse.

That's when she noticed the window.

Patty's reflection was there in the window's dark glass. Her silhouette wasn't a bright ghostly white, but instead composed of darkness and shadows. Almost like she was standing outside in the night, even though Erin's bedroom was on the second floor.

She was in her nightgown, with her blonde curls hanging past her shoulders, and her eyes glowing pearly white.

"What do you want? What *about* Paula?" Erin breathed, pressing her back against the door. Clearly, Patty's unfinished business had something to do with her twin, but Erin had no idea what it was.

Behind her, she gripped the doorknob tightly.

Patty's dead eyes still stared blankly at Erin, then she pressed her hands against the glass. It looked so real, like she was just outside the window. Her breath fogged the glass and she left silver prints as her fingers curled into fists, making a squeaking sound.

"Patty?" Erin whispered. "Tell me what—"

Then the ghost raised her fists and pounded on the glass. To Erin's horror, a crack in the window appeared. Patty's face contorted with rage and she lifted her fists again and banged against the window. But there was no sound except the cracking of glass.

"Stop!" Erin cried.

The ghost banged on the glass again and the crack spider-webbed. A piece even dropped to the floor.

"Erin!" her father's voice called, and then footsteps pounded down the hall. Erin had just enough time to step away before the door was flung open and her father and mother stood at the threshold.

"Erin, what in the world is going on—what happened to the window?"

Erin looked from her parents to the broken window. The ghost was no longer there, only the outline of tree branches could be seen in the dense darkness.

"I—there . . ." Erin stammered. She was going to get in trouble *again*. Was this all part of Patty's plan as well? To drive her and her family apart by constantly getting Erin in trouble?

And though part of her knew she should tell her parents the truth—that it had been the work of a ghost—just like all the other times, she couldn't bring herself to say it.

"I . . . I shut the window too hard."

"Erin!" her father growled with frustration.

"Oh, Erin," her mother moaned.

"I'm sorry! I didn't do it on purpose."

"That's not the point, Erin!" her father snapped. "What did we talk about? This is our house now! We have to take care of our property."

"Stephen," Mrs. Dodgeson began.

But Mr. Dodgeson held up his hand, shaking his head. "No, Laura, this is just one time too many. We've been beyond lenient and understanding. Yes, this move has been hard on all of us, but we can't just keep letting her get away with these things."

A sinking feeling started in Erin's stomach. She knew what was coming next but she had no way of stopping it.

"Erin, you're grounded."

15

Erin had been grounded only once before. It had been for yelling at Becca and making her cry. Erin's temper had just snapped that day—one too many of her things had been ruined by her little sister's carelessness. Looking back on it, Erin felt she deserved being grounded. It's not like she'd *enjoyed* making Becca cry.

But this time, Erin was taking the punishment for things that were absolutely not her fault. Angry and upset didn't even begin to cover what she was feeling. Still, she didn't exactly blame her parents either. She could understand why they'd been so frustrated with her lately. With all of the recent "incidents," Erin was actually surprised she hadn't gotten grounded sooner.

Naturally, with her being grounded, Erin had to tell Tara she wouldn't be able to meet up with her for a while. The worst part was she wasn't even able to text Tara back and forth about the haunting. Being grounded meant she had to give up her phone too.

Probably the *only* good thing that came with the window cracking and breaking was that it forced Erin to go back to sharing a room with Becca. At first, she hated the idea of sleeping with her little sister again, but after three nights in Becca's room, Erin realized that this was a *good* thing.

In the last encounter with the ghost, it became clear that Erin was staying in what was once Patty's room. It seemed that her spirit was connected to her bedroom, in addition to the treehouse. When Erin moved into Becca's room while her window was being replaced, Erin noticed that she was able to finally sleep peacefully. Her little sister's warmth and steady breathing were soothing and they helped lull Erin into a full night's rest. Which, in turn, allowed Erin to stay awake through the day. That meant no naps where Patty could visit Erin's dreams. And no dreams meant no incidents. No incidents meant her parents were much happier.

A whole week went by without any ghost-related experiences. Erin was careful during that time to stay busy by playing with Becca or helping her parents. She found that as long as she was with another member of her family, Patty left her alone.

Or it could've been a number of reasons as to why Erin stopped seeing the ghost. She stayed away from the treehouse, and with the exception of going into her bedroom to change and grab some of her belongings, Erin largely stayed out of her room as well.

It wasn't the solution to her ghost problem, but it helped.

As the days passed, Erin actually began to wonder if Patty was gone entirely. She didn't test it by going to the treehouse or letting herself accidentally take a nap in the middle of the day, but she began to *hope*.

One morning, while Erin was clearing breakfast dishes, her mother placed Erin's phone on the kitchen table.

"Your father and I agreed you've been punished long enough," Mrs. Dodgeson said with a smile.

Erin resisted the urge to snatch it up and text Tara. Instead, she set down the plates, still coated with syrup from waffles, and hugged her mom around the waist. "Thanks, Mom!"

"You're welcome, sweetie. And I hope this has taught you a lesson."

Yeah, don't move into a house with a ghost, Erin thought to herself bitterly. She nodded and her mother ruffled her hair affectionately before turning and heading back up to her office.

As soon as Erin was done cleaning up, she went into the living room and quickly texted Tara that she was available as early as this afternoon. Tara's reply came quickly but it was slightly disappointing. Tara had soccer practice, so they had to plan for tomorrow instead. It was going to be worth the wait though, because Tara offered to show Erin a nature trail around Pemblebrook, which sounded super cool.

The only problem was making sure she could definitely go—ideally without being made to drag her little sister along.

After dinner, while Becca was up in her room, Erin sought out her parents. They were relaxed on the couch, watching a news program of some sort. They turned the volume down as Erin stepped into the living room and leaned over the back of the couch.

"What's up, Erin?" her father asked, one eye still on the TV.

"You remember the girl, Tara, I told you about?" Erin started.

Erin's mom perked up. "Oh yes, Tara Holland. We met her and her parents at the park that Sunday. Remember, honey?"

"Yep," Mr. Dodgeson said, still not fully paying attention.

"Well, Tara invited me to go on a nature trail tomorrow ..."

Her mother nodded. "That sounds lovely."

"Great, so I can go?"

"I don't see why not. You're not grounded anymore."

"Without Becca?" Erin clarified.

At that, Mrs. Dodgeson frowned, and Mr. Dodgeson turned off the TV. With a sigh, Erin maneuvered her way around the couch to face her parents.

They both looked disappointed and Erin had to wonder if she would *ever* make them happy. As long as she resented taking care of Becca all the time, maybe not.

"Why can't your sister go with you?" Mrs. Dodgeson said patiently. "As I remember, it was actually Becca who hit it off well with Tara."

Again, Erin cursed the fact that she couldn't remember that day. It was even more of a reason that Becca couldn't go though. She *needed* to talk to Tara about Patty and the treehouse. What if Patty came back and some other terrible thing happened? Worse, what if Patty really had taken over her body those missing three days—something Erin hadn't actually admitted to herself because it was too frightening—and she could somehow do it again?

The bottom line was that if Becca went on the nature trail, Erin wouldn't be able to talk about the ghost with Tara.

"Please, Mom, it's just for a couple hours."

"But I thought you two were getting along much better," her mother prodded, ever the person who wanted to get to the root of a problem. "We replaced the window in your room three nights ago and you're still in her room. I thought that was a good sign."

Erin couldn't say that she hadn't gone back to her room yet because she believed it to be haunted.

Clasping her hands in front of her, she begged, "I really want it just to be me and Tara. Becca will—" *make it all about her. Shout things too loudly over and over again. And will want to run off the trail. I'll spend most of my time making sure she doesn't get lost . . .* was what Erin *wanted* to say.

Luckily, her father finally spoke up: "Siblings need a break from each other once in a while, Laura. I think it's fine."

"All right," Mrs. Dodgeson said with a sigh. Then she looked at Erin, giving her a sad smile. "I just want you to enjoy being with your sister, Erin. When you get older you'll treasure that closeness. I promise."

"I already enjoy being with her," Erin said quickly, not sure if that was the truth or not. She loved Becca, but that didn't mean she had to love being with her all the time. "So I can go with Tara tomorrow? Can you drop me off at the park?"

"Will it just be the two of you?" Mr. Dodgeson asked.

"I think so," Erin said. "But we're old enough to walk a trail, Dad. And we'll be careful, I promise. I'll have my cell phone and we won't talk to any strangers."

"I want texts on the hour," her father said after a moment of considering it. "You need to make sure to answer your phone immediately whenever I check on you."

"Thank you!" Erin nearly shouted with glee. She felt like jumping into the air in triumph. Then a thought hit her. She really wanted to take her special binoculars on the nature trail with her, but they were still in the treehouse from the last time she went up there. And she *really* wanted to use them on the trail.

She considered asking her father to get the binoculars, but the doctor told them that her wrist had officially healed two days ago. It didn't hurt and it felt strong, so there was no real reason why she couldn't climb up there herself. She supposed that she could claim to be afraid of going up there now since her fall, but that made her look weak. And Erin liked being strong. Even in front of her family.

Not to mention, she didn't want her father saying something like, "You're old enough to walk a trail by yourself, but you're not old enough to climb up to a treehouse?"

As Erin climbed up the stairs, she considered what to do.

The last time I went to the treehouse had been at night and that's when I saw Patty there. Maybe she won't be there in the morning. I'll go then.

∼∼∽

It was just a half an hour before she had to leave to meet Tara at the park. And still, Erin had yet to go get her binoculars.

She'd been putting it off all morning.

And though she didn't want to admit it, it was because she was scared.

Stop being such a scaredy-cat and climb up there already, Erin told herself as she stared up at the great oak tree, eyeing the wooden planks. The leaves ruffled in the nice cool breeze and the gold sunlight warmed her skin. It was a *beautiful* summer day and it seemed to taunt her.

Gritting her teeth, Erin grabbed hold of the first plank and hoisted herself up. *Just go. In and out. You can be fast.*

Encouraged by her own thoughts and the fact that it was so nice outside, she climbed up the tree faster. Before, it had been dark, and that had to make a difference. Not to mention, she hadn't seen a trace of Patty in almost two weeks.

Erin emerged into the treehouse and lifted herself up onto the wooden floor. Instantly an intense cold chill hit her body and her teeth started chattering like a windup toy. A moment too late, Erin remembered that the first time she'd seen Patty had been in the window of the treehouse ... in broad daylight.

It was her last thought before she felt an icy hand grip her shoulder and her vision tunneled to black.

16

When Erin slowly came to, she felt like there was a set of weights on her body. She wasn't sure how much weight—not enough to crush her, but enough to make it hard to move. It was even hard to open her eyes. Her lids were heavy, not with sleep, but with deep fatigue.

She was so *tired*. She wanted to go back to sleep, but there was a little voice in the back of her mind that said, *If you do, you might not wake up.*

At that terrible thought, Erin wrenched her eyes open.

As she feared, she was not back in the treehouse. She was lying in bed, in a familiar yet unfamiliar room. The layout was the same as her room in the new house. The window, the closet, the door—all were in the right spots. But everything else was different. The wallpaper was yellow with little flowers on it. The furniture was a cherry oak with iron knobs. The rug on her floor looked like an antique. It was the same room . . . but from decades ago.

This can't be happening, Erin wanted to scream.

But she knew it actually was happening. She knew it was real, because this had all occurred before when she fell from the treehouse that night.

Why had she been so stubborn? So independent? She should *never* have gone near that treehouse for her stupid binoculars. Now . . .

The door to the bedroom creaked open. A girl's face appeared around the edge. "Patty?"

Erin held her breath as Paula stepped into the room. She looked the same as before. Straight blonde hair parted down the middle and freckles across her nose. Her dress was similar to the last encounter, frilly and old-fashioned. The only thing that was really different was that her warm blue eyes were rimmed red from crying. She held a stuffed teddy bear in her arms—the same one she always seemed to have whenever Erin saw her—and walked over to the bed and sat.

"You're going to be okay, right, Pat?" Paula asked softly, hold-ing the bear to her face and sniffing.

"Paula, listen—" Erin rasped. She paused because she was shocked at how terrible her voice sounded. It was nothing more than a wheeze and the breath that rattled in her chest made it hard for words to come out. "You have to—"

She broke out into a coughing attack that seized not just her chest, but her whole body. Erin curled into the pillows, her entire torso shaking from the force of her coughs.

"It's okay, Pat, don't talk," Paula said, rubbing Erin's arm in soothing strokes. "You'll get better, because Papa finally finished adding the planks to the tree and now we can go up into the treehouse together." Her voice was thick with tears though, as if she didn't actually believe the words she was saying.

Erin was crying herself—with frustration and helplessness. Her vision blurred as hot tears pricked and burned the corners of her eyes and splashed down her eyelashes.

She was trapped in Patty's sick body once again. Which meant that Patty had control over her body back in the real world.

It hardly seemed possible, but Erin knew that it was the

truth. It was why she couldn't remember the three whole days, why her parents said she forgot where things were, why Becca made those strange comments at the park.

Erin hadn't been Erin. It had been Patty then, and it was Patty now.

Through some kind of power that Patty's ghost had, they were switching places. It might be a dream world, or the actual past, but either way, Erin was stuck here. At least until Patty ran out of the ghostly power she used to switch their bodies.

The only clue Erin had right now was Paula. Patty had said her sister's name multiple times, and in each of these visions, or dream sequences, whatever they were—Paula was here. It had to mean something.

"Pau—" Erin coughed hard, but she was determined to try to get words out, no matter how badly it hurt her chest. "Help . . ."

"Do you need water?" Paula asked, her features full of worry as more tears slid down her cheeks. "You already had your medicine for the day . . ."

Erin shook her head, still coughing, unable to stop. Her

chest hurt so bad that it made her whole body ache. Then she felt a soft touch on her arm. She opened her eyes and found that Paula was sliding her teddy bear next to Erin. Paula's eyes were full of tears, and the way she was looking at the bear made Erin believe that the toy meant a great deal to her. It was her security blanket. It was what she clung to when she was in pain or scared, and now she seemed to be giving up her source of comfort so Erin—Patty—could have it.

And though Erin was scared of these twins—scared of ghosts and what was happening—she couldn't help but feel pity for the two sisters. Feel sad for them. They were losing each other. That was clear. Patty was dying, and Paula's heart was breaking because of it.

"You're going to be okay," Paula whispered, more to herself, as she grabbed Erin's hand. It was then that Erin could see just how thin and bony her hand—Patty's hand—really was. Patty's body was wasting away.

Erin tightened her grip, unable to form words, but desperate to have someone stay with her. She wasn't sure what was more terrifying: being in a ghost's body or being in a body bound for death. And were they really any different?

"Don't worry, Pat. I'm not going to leave you. Ever. I promise," Paula whispered, leaning close.

Over Paula's shoulder, Erin could see *her*. Patty stood in the corner of the room, looking just as dead and as frightening as the last time. White eyes, skeletal features, blue lips. She stood there and mouthed Paula's next words:

"And everyone in Pemblebrook keeps their promises."

17

Erin couldn't stand looking at Patty a moment longer. The sight of her made her feverish skin crawl, as if spiders were racing up and down her arms. She found it hard to breathe. And it wasn't just because she was in a sickly body. Panic was threatening to overtake her. What if there was no going back? What if they had switched . . . for good?

Wake up! Wake up! Wake up!

With a whimper, she squeezed her eyes shut and curled up into a ball, Paula's words echoing in her ear.

Everyone in Pemblebrook keeps their promises.

Those words were still lingering in her mind when Erin opened her eyes again. This time, she was in her own room. Her furniture was all back to normal. Her photo collages of places around the world were hung up, her braided rug in place, and cluttered desk of books and *National Geographic* magazines in their spots.

She was back home.

Looking down at her own hands, she could see that she'd returned to her own body as well. Her hands weren't too spindly, and she even had on chipped nail polish that Becca had applied to her nails while she'd been grounded.

While she felt some relief, the panic and fear from the dream still lingered. For the second time, she had passed out in the treehouse and ended up back in her own bed without any memory. Patty had been in her body just like before—she was sure of it. But . . . for how long this time?

Swallowing, Erin rolled over and grabbed for her phone on the nightstand. Thankfully it was still there. Knowing the ghost, she could've thrown it out the window or smashed the screen or something terrible like that.

The date read: Sat, July 15, 7:45 a.m.

Erin gasped and dropped the phone. It fell, luckily, on her covers.

It was an entire week later. A *week*.

The time was getting longer. Did that mean the ghost was

getting stronger each time she took over Erin's body? What if... what if one time they switched, they never switched back? What if Patty replaced Erin entirely?

That couldn't happen. The thought was not just horrible, it was *horrifying*. Being in Patty's sickly body, Erin felt bad for her, but she certainly didn't want to experience her fate—her inevitable death. But how was she going to make these hauntings stop? Stay away from the treehouse and her bedroom the rest of her life? She *needed* to talk to Tara and understand the history of Patty, Paula, and the treehouse.

Tara!

A bad feeling knotting her stomach, Erin opened up her phone and navigated to the text message conversation with Tara.

It was *not* good. On the day they'd been supposed to go on the nature walk, Tara pinged Erin's phone about a dozen times, asking where she was. With each unanswered text, Tara was getting more and more upset.

TARA: You're late. Where are you?

TARA: Are you not coming?

TARA: Helllooooo?

Then her texts transformed to ones of concern.

TARA: Erin, are you okay? Did you get lost?

Finally, Patty had sent her one simple, rude text message:
Leave me alone.

Erin groaned, stuffing the pillow into her face and letting loose a muffled scream. How could she face Tara now? She'd made her mad, worried her, and then most definitely hurt her feelings, thanks to Patty's unbelievably cold response.

Quickly, Erin fumbled through sending an apology:

ERIN: I'm SO SO SO SORRY. It's a really long story. I promise to explain everything. Can we meet up please? I REALLY need to talk to you.

The rest of the morning, and throughout the day, Erin constantly checked her phone for a text back from Tara. No reply came. With each hour, Erin felt worse and worse. How could she make it up to Tara? How could she convince Tara of one of the weirdest things ever?

That an actual ghost had possessed her body?

Erin wasn't sure Tara would ever believe it, but she had to at least try. All day, she thought about what she could do, and she was glad for the distraction because each interaction with her family was stressful. What had Patty said or done that she didn't know about? And how were her actions going to reflect on Erin?

At one point during the day when Erin was checking her phone, her father joked, "Oh, so you remember how to use it this time?"

Erin laughed with him, but a jolt of panic went through her. Of course Patty didn't know how to use a cell phone. She'd been dead for years, maybe decades. Patty probably had no idea what to do with Tara's messages or the cell phone. It didn't give her any excuse for such a rude reply though.

Just like when she was grounded, Erin stuck close to Becca. The little girl made it easy for her to keep busy and not dwell on her ghostly problems. She was constantly a ball of energy and seemed much more glued to Erin than usual. Erin discovered why later when they were up in Becca's room playing with her many stuffed animals.

"Mr. Fuzzy Hooves is glad you're back, Erin," Becca said cheerfully, walking her giraffe across the rug.

Erin, who'd been holding Lady Daisy the elephant, paused. She decided to test her little sister, an idea forming. "What do you mean, Becca?"

Becca glanced at Erin and then back at her stuffed animals. She didn't reply—the same fear that Erin had seen other times when Patty had shown up back on her face.

Erin deepened her tone and spoke in her Lady Daisy elephant voice, "But Mr. Fuzzy Hooves, I never left. I've been me the whoooole time."

For a moment, Erin didn't think she would play along, but Becca moved Mr. Fuzzy Hooves's head back and forth in a shake. "You look like you, Lady Daisy," Becca said in her giraffe voice, which was rough and deep, "and you sound like you, but you're not you."

"Who am I, Becca?" Erin prodded, forgetting to use her Lady Daisy voice.

Becca threw her arms around Erin's middle, pressing her face into Erin's stomach. "Don't go away again, Erin."

Tears pricked Erin's eyes, a flood of emotions rolling through her. She was so relieved that someone—even her five-year-old sister—knew something was wrong. That something evil was happening and that Erin wasn't herself. Her own parents hadn't noticed the change in Erin, but Becca had. She'd never felt more love for her little sister than she did right then.

"I won't, I promise," Erin whispered, stroking Becca's hair. Becca knowing the truth, even if she wouldn't talk about it outright, made Erin feel a little less alone.

It also gave her an idea.

~~~

Pemblebrook Park wasn't as busy on a Monday as it was on a Friday or during the weekend. But with it being the summer, there was still a fair amount of people.

Erin stood next to Becca, holding her hand, and scanned the soccer fields.

Once again, her mother had dropped them off at the park while she went to write at the library. It hadn't taken a whole lot of convincing to do it either. Apparently, Mrs. Dodgeson enjoyed the change of scenery during her hours of drafting and research.

Of course, Erin had a very specific purpose for asking to come to the park. Throughout the weekend, she'd tried, and failed, to get a response from Tara. But she wouldn't give up. And even though she hated the idea of ambushing Tara after soccer practice, she had no other choice.

Erin breathed out a sigh of relief when she saw Tara kick the soccer ball up and down the field. She even managed to score a goal toward the end of practice. Becca cheered for her, and when Tara looked over at them, a scowl crossed her face when she saw Erin.

Her stomach in knots, Erin followed Becca as she ran to Tara on the sidelines once practice was over.

Tara greeted the five-year-old by holding her hands out in a high ten. Becca clapped both of them and grabbed the soccer ball.

"Can I kick the ball? Can I, Tara?"

Tara smiled. "Sure, but not for long, okay?"

"'Kay!" Becca yelled as she grabbed the ball and started kicking it across the field.

Tara turned back to Erin and folded her arms, her expression cold. "What do *you* want? I left you alone, so now you leave *me* alone."

Erin sighed. "That's what I want to explain. It wasn't me. I didn't text you that."

"So who did?" Tara shot back.

"The ghost."

Tara froze. Her brown eyes stared at Erin in total bewilderment. After a few seconds, she shook her head and said under her breath, "Yeah, right. You're unbelievable."

"It's the truth."

"Ghosts can't hold phones, Erin," Tara snapped. "If you're making fun of me because I believe in—"

"Look, if you'd just let me explain," Erin interrupted, "I'll tell you everything." She was so tired of dealing with this on her own. Becca, even if she knew what was going on, was too young to talk to or really help. And her parents would think she was acting out all over again.

Tara picked up her soccer bag and waved for Becca to come back with her ball. "Forget it. You've blown me off one too many times."

As Becca headed back with the ball, Erin stepped in front of Tara, blocking her path. "Please, Tara. You have to help me." Much to her dismay, her voice cracked with emotion. And stress. She couldn't do this alone anymore. She wasn't as strong as she thought she was.

Tara's brows furrowed, her mouth turning down a little. She seemed uncomfortable with how desperate Erin sounded. But she hesitated still, and Erin honestly couldn't blame her.

Then to Erin's surprise and relief, Becca took Erin's hand. "Please don't be mad at Erin, Tara. Patty makes her do bad things sometimes."

Tara's eyes widened. Then she plopped down onto one of the benches, her lips parted in surprise. Slowly, her shock turned into curiosity. Her eyes narrowed. "Okay . . . I'm listening."

18

"She's possessing you," Tara said flatly, her expression unreadable.

Erin nodded. Her voice was practically hoarse from talking so much. She'd told Tara everything. From the moment she saw Patty's silhouette in the treehouse on the first day they'd moved in to waking up a week later with no memory after traveling back in time in Patty's body. Tara had been quiet for most of it. She'd interrupted only a couple times to ask questions, but that had been it.

Meanwhile, Becca was playing on the playground. As soon as she'd realized the two girls were going to talk about the ghost, she ran off to the swings.

"You realize how unbelievable this all sounds, right?" Tara said, raising an eyebrow. "I mean, a *ghost* is possessing you. That's like something out of a horror movie."

"It's more like we're switching places, and why do you think I haven't told my parents?" Erin said with a sigh. "I didn't think you'd believe me either. Becca is the only one who kinda knows what's going on, but she's too scared to really talk about it."

Tara just shook her head. "This is so weird."

"Okay, your turn," Erin said, nudging Tara with her elbow.

"My turn what?" Tara asked.

"Tell me about the treehouse! Do you know what happened to Patty and Paula?"

"Oh." Tara frowned. "There's not a whole lot, but enough for most people in Pemblebrook to believe in Patty."

"Anything might help at this point."

Tara shifted on the bench, turning to face Erin. "Well, the rumor has been around for years and years. Like, when my mom was a kid. She'd heard about it too. Apparently a lot of the kids wanted to play in the treehouse, but whenever they'd go near, a blonde-haired girl would show up. And then vanish seconds later. It was almost like she was . . ."

"Guarding it?" Erin suggested.

"Yeah. Anyway, enough of the kids saw her that it became

not just a rumor, but almost like a fact. Patty haunted her treehouse."

"Is there anything else?" Erin urged. "I already know she haunts the treehouse."

"But do you know *why?*" Tara asked smugly.

Erin frowned, remembering snippets of conversation from her time in Patty's body. Things Paula had said to her. "Because her dad built it for her and that's where her sister got to play?" Maybe Patty haunted the treehouse because that was her unfinished business. Because she wanted so badly to play in it but never got to.

"Because that's where she died."

"She *died* there?" Erin asked, shocked. She remembered how weak Patty's body had been. How had she been able to climb up there?

"Yep. That's where they found her body the next morning. In fact, the other part of the rumor is that her twin sister woke up next to her. They'd been up there together."

Erin shivered. She couldn't even imagine that. Going up to the treehouse with your sister and waking up to find her cold and unbreathing ... it was truly a nightmare.

"That's awful."

"Tell me about it." Tara shook her head. "Anyway, that's all I really know. Pemblebrook has talked about that old treehouse for years, but it was such a tragedy that no one talks about the family or what happened afterward."

That's when it struck Erin. It was so huge and important that she couldn't believe she hadn't thought of it sooner.

"You mean . . . no one knows what happened to Paula? Is she still alive? Do you know when it happened?" Erin asked. It had never occurred to her that Paula could still be alive since Patty was dead. But if it wasn't *too* long ago, there was a chance that Paula could be alive somewhere. That she could know why Patty's spirit couldn't rest in peace.

"Whoa, whoa," Tara said, holding up her hands at Erin's rapid-fire questions. "I said that was all I knew. I don't know what happened to the rest of the family. It's more of a town legend than actual history."

Erin's shoulders slumped. It made sense that maybe once a long time ago people knew what happened to the family, but over the years they simply lost track.

At Erin's crestfallen look, Tara patted her on the shoulder.

"But hey, I'll keep thinking about it. Maybe my mom will know—I can try to ask her. It's a small town, and there might be relatives of the family still around."

"Thanks," Erin said with a small smile. It really did make her feel a lot better now that she was finally talking to someone about it. Even more, that Tara actually seemed to *believe* her.

"I have to go, but I'll text you, okay?" Tara stood and shouldered her soccer bag. "Just answer this time," she said with a wink.

Erin forced herself to smile back. As long as Patty didn't take over her body again, she would.

True to her word, Tara did text Erin. And it was even later that same day, in the evening after dinnertime. Erin had kept her phone by her just in case, and when the message sound went off, her dad eyed her phone. They were all in the living room, Becca and Mr. Dodgeson were playing a card game, Mrs. Dodgeson was on her tablet, and Erin was reading a book.

"I hope you're not spending too much time on your phone, Erin," he warned.

"It's just Tara," Erin said. "I'm not on YouTube, I promise."

Mrs. Dodgeson looked up from her tablet. "Tara? I thought you weren't interested in being her friend."

Erin felt her cheeks heat. It was infuriating that Patty had been living Erin's life and making these decisions as if they were her own.

"No, I am. It was just a misunderstanding. We're good."

Erin's mom hmmed and went back to her tablet, probably thinking about how fast children change their minds. It wasn't that, Erin wanted to tell her. But she held her tongue.

Erin looked at Tara's text:

TARA: I found something! Call me if you have time tonight.

Heart pounding, Erin bolted from her chair, her book sliding off her lap and to the floor. "Can I call Tara real fast? We want to meet up tomorrow."

Mr. and Mrs. Dodgeson exchanged looks, then her dad nodded. "Sure, but keep it to twenty minutes, sweetie."

"Okay!" Erin called over her shoulder as she raced upstairs, already dialing Tara. She was about to walk into her own room, then she thought better of it. She went to Becca's room instead.

"Hello?" Tara's voice came over the phone.

"Hey, it's me," Erin said, breathless from sprinting up the steps. "What'd you find?"

"All right, slow down," Tara said, laughing.

"Kinda living in a haunted house right now, Tara. Wouldn't you be freaked too?"

"Fair point. Okay, so while we were eating dinner I remembered something. A few months ago my great-aunt died and everyone sent my grandparents cakes and casseroles and stuff for the funeral. And I remember them getting this one chocolate cake and saying that the sender had lived through her own tragedies. Then my grandma had said something like, 'Oh, isn't that the woman from that house?'"

Erin didn't really follow. "So?"

"So! There's only one house in Pemblebrook that people talk about having to do with a tragedy," Tara said, her voice growing louder in her excitement. "*Your* house."

Erin caught on. "Can we find out who sent the cake?"

"Way ahead of you," Tara said smugly. "I already went on my mom's Facebook page and scrolled through her recent messages. She spent a bunch of time online thanking everyone for coming after the funeral and for all the food—you know, since my grandparents can't use a computer. Anyway, I found Darlene Wheeler as one of the people Mom sent messages to."

The name didn't ring any bells, but Tara seemed to be on a roll, so Erin didn't interrupt.

"In the message, my mom asked Darlene to tell *her* mom thank you for the chocolate cake. And Erin, guess what Darlene's mom's name is?"

Erin felt the hair on the back of her neck stand up. She whispered the name, just as Patty's ghost had done.

"Paula."

19

Paula was still alive. And the fact that it was possible to even track her down was nothing short of a small-town miracle.

Erin couldn't imagine tracking down anyone in Chicago, let alone finding the distant relative of someone who once lived in her house. But thanks to the Internet and small-town neighborly gestures, they'd managed to find Paula's daughter, Darlene.

"Do you think Darlene would let us talk to her mom?" Erin asked, checking the time. She didn't have long to be on the phone. Her father would check on her in twenty minutes.

"I doubt it. Besides, how weird would that be?" Tara snorted. Then she put on a fake voice, "Hi, you don't know us, but your mom's dead sister is a ghost that sometimes takes over my body."

"Like I would even say that," Erin snapped. "Can't you message her?"

"Are you kidding? I'm not using my mom's Facebook. I could get in loads of trouble."

Erin sighed. She would get in major trouble if she did something like that too. But how could they find Paula? What clues did she have while being in Patty's body? Erin thought hard. There had to be something. She'd seen the past twice now, and seen Patty and Paula in different, old-fashioned clothes. And they said odd phrases like "the bee's knees" and "swell."

When Erin relayed all this to Tara, she replied, "Oh, that's totally old. My great-grandma still uses those words sometimes. And she's in her late eighties. Almost ninety, I think."

Now that Tara mentioned it, the one time Erin visited her great-grandfather, he had said something like "the fuzz" when referring to the police. She remembered it specifically because she'd asked her mother what it had meant later. And now that Erin thought about it, she recalled Paula using that phrase too, during her time in Patty's body.

That meant Paula had to be pretty old at this point. If she

was anywhere near Erin's great-grandfather's age, then she might not live on her own anymore. Erin's great-grandfather was ninety-one and still pretty sharp, but he couldn't move around very well, so he lived in a senior community living center.

"Is there a senior living place in Pemblebrook?" Erin asked.

"Yeah, there is actually," Tara replied, sounding a little surprised. "My great-grandma lives there."

"Do you think Paula might be there?"

"Maybe. Do you think she really would've stayed in Pemblebrook knowing her sister, you know . . . died here?"

"But Darlene still lives here, and she'd want to live near her daughter," Erin pointed out. Also, Erin couldn't help but remember how close the two sisters had been. Maybe Paula had never moved away from Pemblebrook because she couldn't stand to truly leave her sister behind. It was a sad notion.

"Erin! Are you still on the phone?" her father called up the steps.

"Dang, I gotta go," Erin said quickly. "I'll text you tomorrow."

"Okay, bye. And good luck tonight."

If Erin wasn't mistaken, there was a slight trace of worry in her new friend's voice.

~~~~

That night, Erin slept in Becca's room again. She hadn't returned to her room since she woke up after a week of Patty being in her body. She definitely wasn't taking any chances this time. If Patty somehow managed to get ahold of Erin's body again, Erin could be gone for a month. And after that...who knew? Maybe forever.

Maybe she'd be replaced entirely.

The thought of it made her hug Lady Daisy close to her. It wasn't that she needed to sleep with a stuffed animal, but in Becca's bed, it was inevitable. They were everywhere. Strangely, it made her think of the time in Patty's body when Paula had let her borrow her treasured teddy bear. She'd seen that bear more than once—in her dreams, and in the occasions where they switched bodies. And somewhere else...but she couldn't place where exactly.

It took a while, because she was thinking about too many things, but eventually Erin fell asleep. Only to be awoken a short time later by Becca.

Her little sister was pushing against her arm. "Erin. Erin, wake up. Please, Erin."

Groggily she shifted so that a couple of animals fell off and hit the floor. "Mmm... what is it?"

"She's outside."

Erin's sleepy eyes snapped open. Now she was definitely awake. She didn't even need to ask who Becca meant. Erin knew who "*she*" was.

"How do you know?" Erin asked as Becca slipped farther down into the covers, so not even her forehead was poking out.

"I heard her," Becca said, her voice muffled.

And suddenly Erin did too. The creak of footsteps on floorboards... pacing back and forth in front of the door.

Their parents would never do that. It could only be Patty.

Maybe she was upset that Erin wasn't staying in her room. Obviously, Patty wasn't as easily able to get into Becca's room—but now Erin wondered how long that would last. She'd never heard footsteps before. Scratching, tapping in the walls, the doorknob rattling—she was almost used to those things now. But never footsteps in the hallway.

Could Patty's ghost be growing stronger? Just like how

she was able to take over Erin's body for longer periods of time, could her spirit be wandering to different parts of the house? How long before she made her way into Becca's room as well?

"I'm scared, Erin," Becca whispered from under the layers of sheets and blankets.

Erin felt a surge of protectiveness rise in her chest. Though she wanted to tell Becca the truth, which would've been *me too*, she also needed to be brave for her younger sister. As the older sister, it was Erin's job to protect her and look out for Becca. More than that, Erin *wanted* to. Becca had been the one person throughout this whole ordeal who had believed in Erin and made her feel less alone and less helpless.

"It's okay, Becks," Erin murmured, hugging her little sister close. "I'm here."

The footsteps sped up, stomping with such force that the creaks in the floorboards grew louder. Erin gritted her teeth, mostly to stop them from chattering. It was suddenly freezing inside the room. Her breath came out in clouds of vapor. Becca whimpered against her arm.

Summoning her courage, Erin detached herself from Becca

and swung her legs over the bed to stand. It felt like standing on a frozen lake. Her bare feet padded across the wood floor and she stopped in front of the door.

"Erin!" Becca whispered from the bed, her eyes wide with terror.

Erin pressed fingers to her lips and then gave Becca a thumbs-up, as if to say, *It'll be okay.*

With a hard swallow, Erin said loudly, "Go away, Patty."

The footsteps outside the door suddenly stopped.

Erin blinked in surprise. Had that actually worked? Was she gone? It was still freezing, but maybe the temperature would go back to normal in time. Erin hesitated, then placed her hand on the doorknob. It was unlikely that Patty could take over her body. It had only happened when Erin had gone to the treehouse. Her power seemed to be stronger there.

So maybe she could at least check.

Erin opened the door just a fraction and peeked through the crack.

Patty's milky-white eyes stared back. Her blue lips were pulled into a scowl and quick, like a lightning strike, her bony hand shot through the crack and grabbed for Erin's wrist.

With a scream, Erin jumped back, tripping over a stuffed animal and falling to the floor.

The door banged open, and to Erin's relief, her parents were there. Becca threw the covers back and immediately started sobbing. As Mrs. Dodgeson went to comfort Becca, Mr. Dodgeson knelt down in front of Erin.

"Erin? Sweetie, what happened? Why did you scream?"

Erin could only shake her head, too scared to speak.

Her father frowned, looking deeply concerned. Both of his daughters seemed scared beyond words. Clearly they hadn't been goofing off. Whatever had scared them had been truly horrible.

And getting worse.

Because Patty's spirit was stronger. Without a doubt, Erin knew that the ghost was coming for her. And the ghost was losing patience.

20

After a sleepless night, Erin decided that drastic measures had to be taken. There was no way she could survive even one more week in this house. Surely Patty would find a way to take over Erin's body again . . . and for good this time.

Remembering how Patty had tried to grab her hand, Erin had to assume that the ghost took Erin's body by touch. The first time, Patty had clasped her by the wrist when she'd fallen out of the treehouse. The second time, Patty had gripped her shoulder when she went to get her binoculars. That still seemed to be true, but Patty no longer needed to be in the treehouse to do it.

Knowing that, Erin had to do something. Immediately.

Luckily it happened to be a weekday, so the senior living place—Pemblebrook Senior Living—was open. Now that she was so desperate, Erin didn't care about placing a call there without her parents' permission. This was way too important now.

"Hello, it's a lovely day at Pemblebrook Senior Living. How may I help you?" a cheery voice said on the phone.

"U-uh...um," Erin stammered. She hadn't been as prepared as she thought she was. "I—I'm calling to speak to my great-grandma."

"Oh? What's her name, sweetheart?" the cheery woman said kindly.

"P-Paula Wheeler."

There was a pause. "I wasn't aware Mrs. Wheeler had any great-grandchildren."

Erin bit her lip and looked down at Becca. She was coloring in her coloring book, her legs swinging back and forth, totally carefree. Maybe calling hadn't been the greatest idea, but at least she knew that Paula was actually there. That was good news. Really good news.

"She does. When are visiting hours?" Erin asked quickly.

"Mondays through Fridays from nine a.m. to four p.m., and Saturdays and Sundays from eleven a.m. to three p.m.," the woman said, but she sounded less cheery and more unsure.

"Okay, thank you!" Erin squeaked, then she quickly hung up before the woman could ask any more questions. Then she texted Tara.

ERIN: Can you meet at the park at 1 p.m.?

Tara texted back almost immediately.

TARA: I can go at 2.

Erin paused, her thumbs hovering over the digital keyboard. She had to think this through. This couldn't be as unplanned as the phone call, otherwise, she'd never make it in to see Paula Wheeler. However, thanks to Tara, she already had a pretty solid idea as to how to get into Pemblebrook Senior Living. Unfortunately, the real problem would be getting Paula to believe anything Erin said.

It was possible, even probable, that Paula would know about the haunting rumors surrounding the treehouse she used to play in as a little girl. She could even believe that the ghost of her sister actually existed, but to believe that Erin was really switching bodies with her twin? That was way too unbelievable.

Erin had to bring proof. *What* proof though?

"Erin? Can we have a tea party?" Becca asked, interrupting

Erin's thoughts and handing her Lady Daisy. Erin took the stuffed elephant on reflex, but then something made her freeze.

She looked around at all the stuffed animals. Becca had all kinds. An elephant, giraffe, horse, bunny, dog, cat, but...no teddy bear.

It was then that Erin remembered something. It was from weeks ago. The day she'd first gone up to the treehouse. When she had gone through the box of old things from the attic. If she remembered correctly, she had seen...

Without a word to Becca, Erin leapt to her feet. She ran down the stairs, her steps thundering almost as loud as her heart. She grabbed her dad's car keys from the counter and then raced outside to open the trunk.

Please, please, please let Dad still be lazy.

The box her father had been supposed to take to charity still sat in his car's trunk. She remembered it being there because that was when she found the photo of Patty and Paula, after going grocery shopping.

Using the jagged side of the keys, Erin cut open the box and dug through the old junk. With a gasp, she wrenched the teddy bear out from under a pile of musty curtains. It smelled of mothballs, and it was dusty, but it was just as Erin remembered it from her time in Patty's body. This was Paula's beloved bear.

This was her proof.

Erin packaged the box back up and headed to her room. She sat the bear on her desk, snapped a photo of it with her cell phone, and took out the old photo of Patty and Paula, stuffing it into her back pocket.

Paula wouldn't be able to ignore her most precious toy from her youth. She wouldn't be able to ignore the photo, nor anything that only *Patty* should know, which, thanks to her time in Patty's body, Erin now did.

Erin picked her phone back up and texted Tara.

ERIN: See you then

~~~

"You're really lucky this place is five blocks from the park," Tara told Erin as the two girls waited at the street crossing.

Erin had managed to convince Becca to stay home this time. Surprisingly, Becca hadn't put up the least bit of fuss. It helped that Erin was honest with her, and told her that she was trying to stop the ghost from coming back.

So now Erin and Tara were using the map on Erin's phone to

walk from the park to Pemblebrook Senior Living. And Tara was right, if it had been across town, there was no way they could've walked there by themselves and would've had to find a creative way to get their parents to take them there.

"So what are you going to tell the receptionist?" Tara asked as they turned down Bramble Street. "You said that the woman didn't think that Mrs. Wheeler had great-grandkids."

"I was thinking you could tell them we're here to talk to *your* great-grandma instead," Erin said, giving her a sheepish look.

Tara rolled her eyes. "Of course you were. I guess that's fine, but we won't know what apartment Paula is in. We'll have to wander all over the place until we find her. And we have to be back at the park by three thirty for your mom. It's not like we have a lot of time."

Erin massaged her forehead, exhausted from her sleepless night. "I know, I know. Can we ask your great-grandma? Would she know what apartment Paula lives in?"

Tara shrugged. "I don't know. Maybe. For eighty-six, my gamma is pretty sharp—but she may not know Mrs. Wheeler."

"Then we'll just have to search for her," Erin said as they came upon the entrance to Pemblebrook Senior Living.

Erin had to admit, it was a lovely place. Trees with white and pink blossoms lined the well-kept walkway up to the front doors. Four white columns stood in front of the red-brick building with ivy crawling up the sides. The doors were a heavy dark cherrywood that Erin had to use almost all her strength to pull open.

As Tara went up to the receptionist to sign them in to visit her great-grandmother, Erin stayed to the back and kept her mouth shut. She didn't want the receptionist recognizing her voice from the phone call that morning.

The lobby of Pemblebrook Senior Living was just as nice as the exterior of the building. It was decorated in warm colors—a cream plush carpet, with peach armchairs and rustic orange couches. A fireplace was in the corner, and a large wall was full of photos of residents and bulletins of upcoming special events and that month's cafeteria menu. Off to the right she could see that another room—the entertainment room, surely—had a big plasma-screen TV along with several gaming systems. Could the seniors play video games here too?

Erin couldn't help but look around with her mouth slightly agape. When she got older, she hoped to stay in a place like this.

To Erin's frustration, the receptionist insisted on walking them there herself. Apparently the staff didn't want any unaccompanied kids running around. Erin and Tara shared a look as they followed the cheery woman down the hall. How were they going to be able to slip away?

They came to another set of doors that led them out into a courtyard. The courtyard was complete with a fountain and a small pond with a birdbath. Big comfy rocking chairs were aligned under a shaded area, where several old women sat, rocking back and forth and chatting happily.

The receptionist led them to the other side of the courtyard where brass numbers on the wall read 6–10. She opened the door and shepherded Tara and Erin through, then she stopped at a door decorated with a floral wreath. She knocked, and within a few moments, the door opened.

An older Black lady stood at the threshold. Her hair was a steely gray and cropped close to her scalp. She wore large glasses and a shawl, but her eyes were bright with life. "Well, I'll be! Tara!"

"Hi, Gamma," Tara said with a smile.

The receptionist beamed. "Isn't it sweet? I wish more

grandchildren—heck, great-grandchildren!—would visit. Take care, Nellie," she told Tara's great-grandmother.

"Thank you, Betty," the old woman said with a nod as the receptionist headed back to her station. .

"Who's your friend?" Tara's great-grandmother asked, looking at Erin.

"My name is Erin Dodgeson. I just moved to Premblebrook." She held out her hand. "Nice to meet you."

Tara's great-grandmother shook it. Her hand was wrinkly and warm, but her grip was strong. "Nice to meet you too. Come on in."

The two girls headed inside and each took a seat at the couch in the living room. It was a nice little apartment, and well furnished, with several houseplants that brightened up the corners. It was obvious that Tara's family visited often and that her great-grandmother had been here for quite some time.

Tara's great-grandmother reclined in a large armchair and immediately started asking Tara a dozen things. How was her summer vacation? How was soccer practice? Had they won any games? As they chatted, Erin kept checking the clock. Time was ticking by. But how could she slip away? How could she find Paula?

About fifteen minutes into their visit though, Erin spotted something on the fridge. She scooted closer from her spot on the couch and could see that the magnetic paper was a directory of the people listed at Pemblebrook Senior Living.

Erin stifled a gasp when she caught sight of Paula Wheeler with the unit number 5B next to the name.

Now that she knew where to go, Erin just needed an excuse to slip out. "Um, I need to call my mom. I'll just step into the hallway," she said, giving Tara a meaningful look. Tara nodded and distracted her great-grandmother with a story about her skateboarding skills.

Erin hurried out the door and speed-walked down the hall. She had to make it all the way across the courtyard to an entirely different building without being caught or noticed. As she stepped out into the courtyard, a woman in scrubs pushed an elderly man in a wheelchair directly across the way. With a squeak, Erin ducked behind a large potted fern and waited for them to pass by. The man was grumbling about wanting steak for dinner while the woman was patiently explaining to him about his high cholesterol.

Holding her breath, Erin waited until she heard doors close before she raced across the courtyard, past the rocking chairs, to the front building. To her left was a door marked 1–5 in brass letters. She was about to slip through the doors when she noticed another nurse in scrubs unloading her cart with fresh linens and taking them into a room. Holding her breath, Erin waited until the nurse stepped back into the room. Crouching low, Erin rushed down the hall and hid behind the cart of linens just as the nurse stepped back out into the hall. Luckily the nurse was short, so she didn't see Erin on the other side. Erin waited until the nurse went back inside before she swerved around the cart and turned the corner of the long hall.

Finally she came to 5B, the last unit of the building. Other doors were decorated in summer flowers or Fourth of July colors, but this one was rather plain. It looked a little lonely, even.

As she stared at the door, Erin realized she was about to meet the woman from Patty's past. Though Erin had *met* this woman, it had been seventy years ago, when she couldn't have been more than twelve. When she thought about it, it made her head spin.

But she didn't have time to prepare herself. The nurse with the laundry cart could turn down the hall at any second. Erin knocked hard on the door.

For a moment, all was quiet beyond the door. And Erin worried that Paula Wheeler wasn't home today of all days...

Then there were footsteps and the door opened.

An old woman stood in the doorway. Her eyes were blue, but the freckles of her youth were gone, and her hair was white as snow. Wrinkles covered every inch of skin, and when she looked down at Erin, the lines around her mouth deepened.

Before Paula could speak, Erin blurted, "Hello, Mrs. Wheeler. My name is Erin Dodgeson and I just moved to Pemblebrook and I was wondering if I could...um...ask you a couple of questions."

Paula looked at Erin for a long moment. Her blue eyes were clear and bright like the sky, just as Erin remembered them from Patty's memories. And they were sad, just like that day too. Though not rimmed with red—now they were framed by wrinkles.

She heaved a deep sigh and said, "You're here about Patty, aren't you?"

21

Silence stretched through the hallway of Pemblebrook Senior Living. Erin stood there in shock, staring up at the old woman.

"Well, come in," huffed Paula as she turned her back and headed into her apartment.

Erin hurried to follow her inside before the old woman changed her mind.

It was a nice place, though not very well decorated. It had the same layout as Tara's gamma's unit, but flipped. The walls were painted a soft yellow, and the furniture was a mixture of different styles, obviously accumulated through the long years. There were a few photos on the walls, but only seemed to be of one family. A younger Paula, a man, and then a boy. Then the boy seemed to have grown up to have a family of his own. He'd married a girl with red hair and Erin had to assume that the woman was Darlene. So Darlene was actually Paula's daughter-in-law. Judging from more pictures, it looked as if Paula had two college-aged grandchildren, but Erin could only guess.

Paula settled back into a very large maroon armchair, then she gestured Erin toward the sofa. "Take a seat," she said in a weary voice, like she knew this conversation was going to take a toll on her.

Erin shuffled over and sat on the sofa, which was a little small and a little threadbare, but still worn-in and comfortable.

There was a long awkward moment of silence when Erin realized maybe she should be speaking. Though she was still getting over her shock that Paula had known immediately why she was here. Perhaps the idea of Patty's ghost weighed more heavily on her mind than Erin had even thought.

"Um . . ." Erin started.

"Let me guess," Paula interrupted, fixing Erin with her blue stare, "you moved into my old house."

Erin could only nod.

"And you've seen Patricia."

Erin had never known Patty's full name, but it made sense. It was a pretty name too.

"So why are you here? To tell me stories of you seeing her ghost wander the halls? To depress an old woman by making her remember her dead sister?" Paula said. Her voice wasn't harsh, or even angry, though her words sounded a bit cold. If anything, she just sounded tired. Tired and sad.

"No, it . . ." Erin swallowed thickly, balling her hands into fists. She knew this was going to be a difficult conversation. "No, I want to help her find peace. I want to put her spirit to rest so she's not haunting my house anymore."

Paula made a sound in the back of her throat, bordering on a laugh. "She hasn't found peace in seventy years. Why would now make any difference? Just tell your parents to move. Maybe they've seen her too," Paula said with a wave of her hand.

"Aren't you upset your sister is a ghost?" Erin asked, unable to stop herself.

Paula laughed, but there was no joy in the sound. Her gaze looked off into the distance as she murmured, "Upset. What a simple word for the way I feel."

"Then how *do* you feel?" Erin pushed. She knew that Paula was the key somehow. Patty wouldn't have mentioned her name or revealed most of her memories with Paula if she wasn't important. Something had happened between the two of them and they carried it with them ever since, following Patty in death, haunting Paula in life.

Paula's gaze shifted to Erin, then she shook her head and started to get up from her armchair. "I think you should leave now. I'm in no mood for ghost stories today."

"She's taking over my body," Erin said.

Paula froze in getting up, looked at Erin, and then slowly lowered herself back down. "She's . . . she's what?"

"It started when I went into the treehouse. Now when I fall asleep, she comes to me in my dreams and makes me do things," Erin said quickly. "But it's gotten worse, and she's possessed my body twice. Her ghost touches me and suddenly I'm in *her* body back when she was really sick, and then I wake up days later in mine and can't remember anything. Please, Mrs. Wheeler, you have to tell me how to make your sister go away. I don't want Patty taking over my body ever again!"

Paula's face was a grim mask of anger. She clutched the arms of her armchair so hard that her knuckles turned ghostly white.

"Didn't your parents tell you it's bad to lie? Now leave. Leave, or I'm going to call someone to get you," she said hoarsely, her voice thick with emotion.

But Erin didn't budge. Instead, she pulled out the photo of the two of them and passed it to Paula. Paula took it with shaky fingers, staring at the photo, her already-pale skin going terribly white.

She swallowed and shook her head, dropping it into a wrinkled hand. "Just an old photo. This proves nothing."

"You both used to play cops and robbers," Erin said as she fumbled for her cell phone. She had to pull out her proof.

Paula pounded the armchair. "Leave!" she shouted, tears glistening in her eyes.

Erin flinched and stood, but she had one last thing to try. "Okay, I'll go, but please look at this." She brought up her cell phone, showing the picture of the teddy bear. "I found your bear in a box of old junk. You gave it to Patty when she was at her sickest, even though I know you loved it so much."

Paula gave a sharp intake of breath when she saw the photo of her old teddy bear.

Emboldened, Erin kept going. "You told her everything was

going to be okay, and that you'd never leave her and that... everyone in Pemblebrook keeps their promises."

"What did you say?" Paula looked from the photo to Erin, eyes wide, wrinkled cheeks wet with tears.

"That's what you told her," Erin said. "Everyone in Pemblebrook keeps their promises."

Paula heaved a deep sigh and drew a trembling hand to her forehead. "Oh, Patty, after all this time..."

"Please, Mrs. Wheeler. Something happened between the two of you, and it's something she can't let go of. You have to tell me what it is," Erin pleaded.

Paula gestured for Erin to sit back down, and hesitantly she did.

"Patty was... well, she was always very sick," Paula began slowly. "Her immune system was weak. Every cold, flu, virus, she seemed to catch. But we were very close. We did everything together. We were twins, after all. We shared everything. Clothes, toys, even our first love. His name was Bradley." A faint, sad smile crossed her lips. "But one spring she caught pneumonia and it grabbed hold of her like nothing else. She couldn't shake it, and she and I both knew that it was different this time.

Our father built a treehouse for us, and I think it was partly because he wanted to convince himself that one day Patty would be well enough to play in it.

"But even once the treehouse was built, Patty only got worse. We spent many days in her room talking, and a few times, as awful as it sounded, we talked of death." Paula paused, she cleared her throat, and then pushed forward. "Patty was scared, you see. And why wouldn't she have been? We're all scared of death, though I think once you get to my age, a little less so. I . . . I wanted to do anything to ease my sister's fear. I swore I'd never leave her, that we'd always be together. I told her that if she died, then she could come back to me and we'd meet in the treehouse and we could share my body."

Paula took a deep breath and squeezed her eyes shut, as if remembering something painful.

"It was a silly, childish thing to promise," she continued. "But we shared everything else, why not a body? Besides, I don't think I actually believed it was possible anyway. But it seemed to give her comfort. Then one night, Patty woke me up and asked if we could go up to the treehouse. I told her we shouldn't, that it was dark and we should wait till morning, but she was insistent. So we went up there. She took my bear with her that night. Ever since I'd given it to her, she'd kept it with her. As she was falling asleep next to me, I heard her breathing begin to slow. I don't think I understood what was happening at the time, but it scared me. Like a coward, I climbed down from the treehouse and went to get my parents. By the time they got up there... she had passed on. I never went back up though. Never... again."

Paula's story left Erin speechless. It was so sad, and yet terribly frightening too.

"So, Patty was waiting for you..." Erin said softly.

"Yes," Paula said sadly. "And I think she might be to this day."

"Do you think... if she saw you again that her spirit could finally rest in peace?" Erin asked gently.

Paula looked away, out the window. Her gaze was distant and heartbroken. She didn't answer Erin's question, and instead said, "Would you bring the bear to me? I'd like to have it."

Erin licked her lips, knowing it was a cruel, selfish thing to ask. "Maybe you could come get it?"

Paula said nothing, then she looked away from the window

back to Erin. Her voice was cold and firm, but Erin could hear the pain underneath. "You should go."

Erin knew she had pushed her too far already. So without another word, Erin headed out of the apartment and back to Tara's great-grandmother's place, not caring if she got discovered this time. As she walked across the courtyard of Pemblebrook Senior Living, Erin couldn't help but feel even more hopeless than before. Paula seemed to want nothing to do with Patty's ghost. She was full of regret and deep *fear.*

So even though Erin had gotten her questions answered, giving Patty what she wanted was still impossible. They couldn't go back in time and change what had happened. Patty was trapped forever in that treehouse until she found a new body.

And, technically, she already had.

22

As Erin and Tara neared the entrance of the park, they noticed that their parents' cars were parked close together. Shooting each other nervous glances, they hurried over to where their mothers were chatting happily.

"Think they noticed we weren't at the park?" Tara asked as they jogged over.

"Maybe. They look pretty distracted though," Erin said.

Sure enough, Mrs. Dodgeson and Mrs. Holland seemed to be in the middle of making plans and didn't even notice when Tara and Erin approached.

"Oh, we'd love to have dinner tomorrow night," Mrs. Dodgeson gushed. "Stephen and I have been so busy with the new house and moving, and his new job. It's been exhausting. A night out is exactly what we need."

"Fantastic," Tara's mom said, clapping her hands. "We'll go to that Italian place I was telling you about. They have this hand-made pasta that's to die for and the deserts are *amazing*."

Erin knew from experience that when adults talked this happily about something, children were almost never invited. Tara and Erin exchanged looks, as if they both knew that tomorrow night they'd be stuck at home heating up leftovers or something.

"If you guys are going out to dinner, can I go to Erin's house?" Tara jumped in.

Erin could've hugged her in that moment. Not only would it be her first night with a new friend, but if her parents were going to be gone after dark, then it would've been just her and Becca left at home. With a ghost.

This way, Tara could be with them, and it made her feel just a bit better.

Erin's mom beamed. "I think that's a wonderful idea."

"Absolutely," agreed Mrs. Holland. "We'll come over and drop Tara off and pick you and Stephen up, and then the four of us can ride together to the restaurant."

"How does seven sound?" Mrs. Dodgeson said, opening the car door for Erin.

"We'll see you then," Mrs. Holland said with a wave as she and Tara headed for their car.

As Mrs. Dodgeson steered the car toward home, she told Erin cheerfully, "I'm glad you changed your mind about Tara, sweetie."

Erin wanted to tell her she'd always liked Tara but couldn't, so she only smiled weakly.

～⌒⌒

As Erin was brushing her teeth before bed, Becca came up behind her, clutching Mr. Fuzzy Hooves to her chest. "Hey, Erin?"

Erin spat the toothpaste in the sink and wiped her mouth with a towel. "Yeah?"

"Do you think she'll come again tonight?"

When Erin had gotten home from the park, Becca hadn't asked her anything about the ghost. Becca seemed to only want to talk about her when it was necessary. And even then, she looked extremely uncomfortable and frightened.

"Don't worry, Becks," Erin said, ruffling her little sister's hair. She didn't want to lie to Becca, but she didn't want to frighten her either. "I'll protect you."

Erin held out her hand to her little sister and Becca took it. Together they walked back to Becca's room and got into bed. Becca snuggled against her and Erin draped her arm over her. Not for the first time, Erin felt a little guilty about resenting Becca so much in the past. Maybe her baby sister was annoying and loud sometimes, but she was sweet and loved Erin to pieces. The feeling was mutual.

Erin lay awake listening to her parents' movements in the other bedroom, and then the telltale sounds of doors closing. She turned on her side and watched the lights from under the door vanish and darkness take its place.

The house was still.

Erin pressed her lips together, listening hard. Maybe Patty wouldn't come again tonight, but Erin very much doubted it. Now that Patty was strong enough for her spirit to roam around the house, the hauntings would only get worse.

Next to her, she could feel Becca's breathing change into something slow and even. It made Erin think of Paula's story, about being up in the treehouse as Patty was taking her final breaths . . .

She couldn't imagine going through that with anyone, much

less her sister. How scared Paula must've been. It wasn't her fault that she ran away that night. Any kid would've. But how long had Paula dealt with the guilt of never facing her sister's spirit and her final wishes? From her reaction earlier today—the sadness and weariness all over her face—probably not very well.

Erin was on the cusp of sleep when she heard the creaking.

It was faint, so faint that Erin wondered if it was coming all the way from the stairs. Then it slowly got louder as, step by step, Patty stalked down the hall toward their room.

Erin held her breath, her heart pounding, as she struggled to come up with something to do. Maybe Patty would go away as soon as Erin called for her parents. But she didn't want to.

The footsteps grew closer, and the doorknob began to slowly turn. The temperature dropped in the room and Becca shivered next to her.

Why are you being so stubborn? Erin told herself. This wasn't about being brave, this was about Patty reaching her and taking over her body again.

Just as Erin was about to jump from the bed and shout for her parents at the top of her lungs, she saw something out of the corner of her eye. She turned her head and gasped.

Patty was standing at the end of the bed.

Her ghostly form was transparent in the moonlight coming in from Becca's window. Her blonde curls looked silver, but her eyes were as empty and as white as ever. They drew Erin in and much against her will—just like those times in her dreams—she found herself compelled to follow. To obey. She began to lean forward . . . toward Patty's outstretched hand.

Becca screamed.

It was so shrill and loud that it snapped Erin out of whatever ghostly trance she seemed locked in. In seconds, the door burst open and their parents came in.

Becca was back to sobbing and Mrs. Dodgeson once again rushed to comfort her. "Becca, honey, what is it?"

Becca could only shake her head and continue to cry, big fat tears rolling down her cheeks. Mrs. Dodgeson picked her up and carried her out, shushing her and stroking her hair.

Mr. Dodgeson sat heavily on Becca's bed, his shoulders slumping in defeat. "Just what is going on, Erin?" he said, his voice exhausted. "This is the second night in a row. Is it bad dreams? We thought it was a good thing you girls wanted to sleep together, but maybe you need to be in your own beds again."

"No," Erin said quickly. "Becca's scared. We both are. She needs me."

Erin's father ran a hand through his bedhead hair and looked at her with a deep frown. "Scared of *what*? What aren't you telling us?"

Erin looked down at her hands. They were shaking slightly. That had been too close. Becca had saved her with her scream. In the end, Becca had protected her, not the other way around.

"Listen, Erin," her father began, rubbing a comforting hand up and down Erin's back. "Your mother and I pay more attention than you think we do. We know something strange has been going on with you. You've never acted like this before. Acting up and lashing out, changing your personality and your tastes practically overnight. We don't claim to know everything about parenting, but please know that you can tell us anything. You've always been so independent. But you don't have to be."

"Dad, do you believe in ghosts?" she asked softly.

Her father's brows knit together, then his expression turned thoughtful. "Well, I don't know what happens after we die, so anything is possible, I suppose. But more than that, I believe that our minds are complicated machines. And sometimes they create things when we're stressed."

It wasn't exactly the answer Erin was looking for. And she could tell that if she told him now about the ghost, he would try to make sense of it. Make an explanation for something that defied explanation.

So instead, Erin swallowed down the truth and leaned against her father's side. "Can Becca and I sleep in your room tonight?"

Her dad sighed, but he kissed the top of her head. "Sure you can, sweetie. But this has to stop, you know?"

Erin agreed. This did have to stop. But how?

23

The next day Erin was a nervous wreck. It was all she could do to keep from pacing the house and almost bursting into tears after what had happened last night. She was sure that if Becca hadn't woken up and screamed in that exact moment, Erin would no longer be *Erin* anymore.

Somehow Patty had lured her in with her creepy eyes and ghostly power. Apparently, Erin didn't really need to be asleep for that to work. Patty's powers were growing with every day that they lived in this house. The only thing that seemed to stop her was the presence of an adult.

Erin wasn't sure why. The best she could guess was that maybe for Patty to fully replace Erin, the Dodgesons needed to believe that Erin was still their daughter. Why else would Patty vanish every time they entered the room?

Of course, realizing that, it only made Erin worry more. Because her parents would be gone tonight. Sure, Tara would be there, but would that stop Patty? Erin had a sinking suspicion that it wouldn't.

How could she stop her parents from leaving? Pretend to be sick with a stomachache? And what would that solve for the future? It wasn't as if they could live like this forever. Sleeping in her parents' bedroom, faking being sick so they would never leave. Her parents would *truly* think something was wrong with her then.

Seven o'clock, the time for her parents to leave, was quickly approaching and Erin knew she had to do *something*. Even knowing that it was probably a lost cause, she kept thinking about yesterday and Paula's sad story. The pain on the old woman's face was so real that Erin knew Paula must have regrets. She promised to always be there for her sister, but left at the moment Patty had needed her most.

Of course, Erin couldn't blame her. It was a cruel and terrifying thing to ask someone to face death. It was understandable for Paula to have run away.

Except now Erin and her own sister were suffering because of it.

With that thought, Erin snatched up her phone and redialed the number she'd called yesterday morning. The cheery receptionist, Betty, answered. "It's a lovely day at Pemblebrook Senior Living. How may I help you?"

Erin licked her lips. "Um, I—I'd like to talk to Paula Wheeler, please."

Betty paused. "Who may I ask is calling?"

"Uh, my name is Erin Dodgeson. She knows me. Please, I just need to speak to her."

The pause was even longer, then Betty said in a gentle voice. "I'm sorry, sweetheart, but Mrs. Wheeler had a rough night last night. I don't think she's up for talking to anyone."

Erin sighed, her shoulders falling a little. "Okay, can you give her a message for me?"

"Sure, honey. What is it?"

"Tell her..." Erin swallowed. She was going to beg her to come to her old house. To finally face her sister after all these years. But how could she ask that of someone so old and frail? Erin could see that regret was its own ghost. And maybe Paula had been haunted long enough. She shouldn't be punished for being a child. For being scared.

"Tell her that ... Pat forgives her."

Half an hour before Tara and her parents were supposed to arrive, Erin found her mother in the bathroom, putting on makeup in the mirror. She leaned against the doorway and tucked her hands in her pockets.

"Do you have to go tonight?" Erin asked.

Mrs. Dodgeson looked at Erin in the mirror. She smacked her lips with newly applied lipstick and gave her a frown. "Is something wrong, Erin?"

"No," Erin replied shortly. "I just ..."

"Honey, I thought you'd be happy with Tara coming over. Is this because you have to watch Becca?"

Erin just looked down at her feet, nudging her toes under the bathroom rug.

Mrs. Dodgeson tapped her makeup brush against the rim of the blush she was applying. "We ordered you girls pizza. You can watch a movie. It won't just be easy, it will be fun too." Then her mother leaned down and kissed her on the top of the head, like her father had done last night. "I promise."

As her mother retreated into her closet to get her high heels, Erin muttered under her breath, "And everyone in Pemblebrook keeps their promises."

❦

The Hollands arrived at seven on the dot. Their car rolled onto the long driveway just as Mr. Dodgeson was paying the pizza delivery guy.

The adults commented on how nice they all looked, then kissed their daughters goodbye—reminding them to keep the door locked and that they would call around nine before they headed home.

Erin watched the car pull away and onto the road, the tires crunching on the gravel driveway. She wanted desperately to run out and chase after the car, beg them not to go. Instead, she flopped down on the couch next to Tara. Becca was already chewing on a piece of pepperoni pizza and humming to herself as she colored a drawing of a fairy.

"So how was last night?" Tara asked.

Becca hummed louder. Erin gestured for Tara to move to the

kitchen and she spoke in a low voice. "Sorry, Becca doesn't like to talk about it. She's super scared."

"I don't blame her," Tara said with a shiver. "And just so you know, I don't exactly want to be here, but if I were you, I'd be scared out of my mind to be here alone..."

Erin was truly touched and she almost hugged Tara. "Thanks for being here. I mean it, Tara."

Tara's cheeks reddened as she shrugged. "Don't mention it. Let's just figure out what to do about this ghost, right?"

Erin groaned, dropping her head into her hands. "I have *no* idea what to do. Maybe Paula was right. Maybe I should convince my parents that we need to move. They'll *hate* that though. They spent so much time and work on this house. But I think I'm really running out of time."

"What makes you say that?" Tara asked.

Erin quickly relayed what had happened last night. "I felt the same way I had in those dreams," she finished. "Like I was compelled to do it. I don't know ... like she was hypnotizing me or controlling me or something."

Tara shivered again. "That's *really* creepy."

"Tell me about it. If Becca hadn't screamed . . ." Erin trailed off, not even wanting to think about it.

Tara turned to the pizza box on the counter and took a slice. "Maybe we could try talking to Paula again," she said around a mouthful of pepperoni and cheese. "I know you told me she didn't take it very well, but if there's a chance, it's worth a shot."

Erin grabbed a slice too. "Actually, I called her this afternoon."

"*What?* What did she say?"

"I couldn't get to her. So I left a message."

"What message?"

Erin shook her head. "It doesn't matter. I don't think she can help anyway."

"Erin!" Becca shouted from the living room. "Can we watch *Ladybug*?"

Erin resisted the urge to roll her eyes. "Okay, just a second!"

Tara gave her a questioning look.

"You'll see," Erin answered with a laugh.

～～

Two episodes into a teenage superhero show later, the sun had finally set. Becca was already sleeping. She had curled up with

Lady Daisy tucked under her arm after eating her second and a half slice of pizza and conked out.

Erin turned off the TV and checked the time. It was around eight. They still had an entire hour before their parents made it home. But . . . so far, so good. Maybe she'd just been incredibly paranoid all day.

"Let's take a look at your room," Tara said, suddenly getting to her feet.

"What? Why? You know that was Patty's room."

"Exactly. Maybe there's some kind of clue in there that will help us. A message scratched into the wall, like in the treehouse."

Erin shrugged. She didn't think it would actually help anything, but she appreciated Tara trying. It meant a lot. So she stood and moved a blanket over her sleeping little sister, then headed upstairs with Tara.

They entered her room, which Erin hadn't really been in for longer than five minutes for over a couple weeks now.

"Whoa! Cool photo collage!" Tara said, rushing over to the wall that Erin had so meticulously arranged.

"Thanks," Erin said with a smile.

The two girls spent a few minutes talking about the places within the photos and which countries they wanted to visit when they got older. Tara only interrupted the conversation to complain that the room was too cold.

Erin turned away from the photos, realizing that yes, it had gotten significantly colder in here. Which usually meant...

"Hey, that's cool," Tara said, looking at the old globe on Erin's desk. Erin glanced at the globe—she'd almost completely forgotten about it. It was then the globe slowly started to turn on its own. Just like the first night of the haunting...

Tara did what Erin had done that night. She held out her hand to check for a breeze from the air conditioner. "Nothing's blowing. Then how is it moving? And why is it so cold in here?"

The reality of what was happening hit Erin like a ton of bricks. In fact, she expected Patty's ghost to suddenly appear any moment.

"Erin?" Tara whispered, her eyes wide, as if she too was beginning to realize that this was the work of Patty.

Something, and Erin wasn't sure what it was—maybe an older sister's intuition—made her look out the window.

Down below, in the backyard, Erin saw them. Walking across the grass in the light of the full moon was her little sister, Becca, still holding her stuffed elephant. She was following a transparent girl in a nightgown with blonde curly hair.

Going straight toward the treehouse.

24

"BECCA!" Erin screamed. Without a plan, or even a second thought, Erin bolted out of her bedroom and raced down the stairs. Vaguely, she was aware of Tara's steps behind her, but she was too focused on getting to her little sister.

She was supposed to watch over Becca—protect her. And now Patty had her. Maybe Patty had gone for Becca because Erin had proven too hard to replace? It didn't matter now. The only thing that mattered was getting Becca back. Because what if Patty became so strong that she took over Becca's body forever? Patty probably wouldn't need any "trial runs" this time, since she was obviously way stronger.

Erin would never be able to live with herself if she let that happen.

These awful thoughts ran through her mind as she flung

herself at the back door and tried to pull it open with shaking hands.

But it didn't budge.

Erin checked the lock. Becca had come out this way, so of course it wasn't locked, but why wasn't it opening? Another result of ghostly powers?

"Let her go, Patty!" Erin shouted at the ceiling. "Let her go now!"

The lights in the hall and the rest of the house started flickering. An electric buzz echoed through the walls as the lights went off and on, throwing both Erin and Tara into the shadows.

"Erin . . ." Tara started. She had Erin by the shoulder. Whether it was out of support or fear, Erin didn't know, maybe both. But she couldn't answer Tara when Becca was probably almost up in the treehouse by now.

"You can't have her!" Erin continued to shout. "Leave her alone, you stupid ghost!"

A terrible loud banging started, and Erin ran back into the kitchen to find the cupboard doors opening and slamming shut. Pots started rattling on the shelves. Their metallic clanking and the bangs of wood against wood filled the house with noise.

"You can't shut me up!" Erin screamed over the racket. "You know this is wrong, Patty! You lived your life. You can't take Becca's!"

The lights started flickering faster, the air got colder, the drawers in the kitchen slammed in and out, and the cupboard doors banged harder. Even the furniture in the living room started vibrating. Then the lights went out for good, and the girls were plunged into darkness.

It would've been terrifying, and Tara definitely found it so— she had Erin's arm in a death grip—but the only thing that scared Erin was losing Becca for good.

"Leave Becca alone!" Erin cried again, feeling around underneath the sink. She grabbed what she'd been looking for and turned on the flashlight. A gold beam shot through the darkness to the ceiling, but it only made the shadows more sinister.

The shadows in the corners stretched and stretched until they looked like long streaks of black ooze. It reminded her of her nightmares. How they tried to drown her and smother her and overtake her. They had tried to erase every part of Erin, making her nothing but an empty shell for Patty to enter.

"I'm sorry Paula wasn't there for you! I'm sorry you had to

die! But that doesn't mean you can take my little sister. This is wrong, Patty! You *know* it is!"

"Erin! Look! Look!" Tara cried, pointing to the back door down the hall. A stream of moonlight cut through the darkness.

It had creaked open.

Erin gasped with relief and sprinted down the hall, out the door, and into the backyard. Maybe her words had gotten to Patty's spirit somehow. Maybe there was a part of her that was still human and knew that what she was doing needed to be stopped. Erin had to believe that, because that was the only hope she had to save her sister.

The full moon was bright enough so Erin could see where she was going. She raced over the grass barefoot, stepping on a broken branch and a sharp rock more than once, but she didn't stop. Even when she heard the sound of a car pulling into the driveway, and saw the headlight beams illuminate the backyard in gold, rather than the supernatural silver of the ghost. In the back of her mind, she prayed the car was her parents home early. But she didn't stop to check, she just kept running toward the treehouse.

Shaking, tears running down her cheeks, Erin grabbed hold of the first plank and started climbing. She climbed faster than she ever had before in her life, and in seconds she had pulled her body through the hole in the treehouse floor.

She collapsed on the dusty wood, finding Becca's body lying beside her. Erin grabbed her sister by the hand and, trembling, raised her head to look up at the ghost standing over them.

Patty was more solid than she'd ever looked. Her outline was glowing with a silver light and her eyes were no longer as milky—they were clear and blue. Like her sister, Paula's. Her lips were still blue, and her cheeks were still sunken, but she looked more alive . . .

"I'm here," Erin said in a shaky voice. "You can take me now. Not Becca."

Patty tilted her head, her expression still icy. But . . . there was something in her gaze. Something that hadn't been there before.

"Do you understand what I'm saying?" Erin said slowly, get-
feet and taking a step toward Patty. "Take my body
ister's. Please."

hesitate.

Next to Erin, Becca stirred. She picked her head off the floor. "Mmm...what? Erin?" Then she recoiled at the sight of Patty's ghost and immediately began sobbing in terror.

Erin felt like crying herself but she kept her gaze on the ghost. "Let me get Becca down safely, okay? Then I promise, you can take my body."

Patty's blue eyes narrowed.

Then Erin said the words that she knew Patty would believe. "Everyone in Pemblebrook keeps their promises."

Finally, the ghost nodded. With a breath of relief, Erin helped Becca down through the hole in the treehouse floor. Tara was there, making sure Becca was steady as she climbed down the old wooden planks.

Once Erin was on the grass as well, Patty's ghost suddenly appeared next to her. Tara gave a sharp cry as she saw the ghost for the first time herself. Becca whimpered, and clung to Tara. But Patty's icy-blue gaze locked onto Erin's, as if to say, *You promised.*

She held out her ghostly hand.

Erin knew she had to take it.

For Becca.

"Tara, take Becca inside. Please."

Tara looked like she wanted to argue, but didn't. She tried dragging Becca away, but the five-year-old was sobbing and shouting Erin's name.

Erin tried to block out Becca's cries as she reached out to grab Patty's hand.

Then an older voice shouted across the backyard, *"PAT!"*

25

Erin and Patty both looked over as a silver-haired old woman limped down the porch of the house.

It was Paula Wheeler. Erin couldn't believe it. Was that who had arrived in the car? It hadn't been her parents coming home, but Paula—maybe taking a taxi all the way here. But why had she come? Had Erin's message had the opposite effect? By telling Paula that her sister forgave her, maybe that had made Paula realize that forgiveness was what she'd been looking for.

Neither sister could move on until they faced each other.

Paula Wheeler moved carefully across the grass toward the old oak tree. Her chest rose and fell with effort as if moving as quickly as she could had taken all the strength she had left.

"Pat," Paula said softly, her blue gaze focused on the ghost of her twin. "I'm sorry it took me so long."

Patty stared at Paula, and Erin felt like she was intruding on a very intimate family moment. But she dared not leave.

"You waited so long for me," Paula said, tears leaking out of the corner of her eyes and rolling down her cheeks. She held out her old weathered and wrinkled hands. "And I never came. I'm sure that hurt you. Warped you into something you're not. But I'm here now. We can play here. Together. Forever."

For the first time, Patty's expression wasn't one of anger or coldness. The ghost looked tormented, and truly in pain. It looked like she wanted, more than anything, to be able to talk to her sister at long last. But there was only so much her ghostly powers could allow.

It was at that moment that Erin knew what she had to do. *This* was Patty's unfinished business, and Erin had known all along she would have to help her somehow.

Without hesitation, Erin held out her hand, and a grateful smile flicked across Patty's face as she took Erin's hand.

Strangely, it was not the intense feeling of cold that she had felt in the past when touching the ghost. This time, it was warm. Gentle. Almost a bit like standing in a patch of sunlight through a window.

She felt Patty's spirit take control of her body, but unlike the instances before, Erin's vision did not fade to black. Instead, she felt merely displaced. Out of her own body, but still present and aware of the world around her.

Erin watched, in both shock and awe, as her body stepped forward and wrapped her arms around Paula's middle. And though it was Erin's voice, it was Patty who said, "I missed you, P."

At first, the old woman looked just as shocked, but then her lips turned into a soft smile. "I missed you too, Pat. Thank you for waiting for me."

It happened suddenly—like the blink of an eye—but Erin was back in her body once again. She was still hugging Paula, and more surprised than anything else, Erin let go.

"I think she's gone," Erin said, looking around them for any signs of the ghost.

Mrs. Wheeler took a deep breath. "Yes, I do hope so. She deserves to finally rest after all this time." Then the old woman patted Erin gently on the shoulder. "Thank you, my dear," she said softly.

Erin blinked, confused. "For what?"

She was still reeling after everything that happened. She was glad Patty was gone, but it had happened so fast. Maybe seeing Paula again and holding her twin one last time had been all she had needed.

"For saving this old woman," Paula continued with a soft chuckle. "I was finally able to keep my promise."

"Erin?" Tara called from the porch. Becca was standing next to her as well, holding tight to her hand. "What happened? Is Patty gone?"

"She's gone," Mrs. Wheeler said. "It doesn't look like your parents are home, so let's go inside and wait. Maybe one of them can give me a lift home."

~~~

The rest of the evening was a whirlwind. When their parents finally came home, just ten minutes after nine, the adults were more than a little surprised to find a strange old woman with the girls. Mrs. Wheeler had blamed it on her old age, explaining that this had once been her house and she had gotten confused. Erin's and Tara's parents ended up believing it, of course, and were more concerned about Paula Wheeler's health than anything else. And as Mrs. Wheeler had predicted, Mr. Dodgeson ended up driving her back to Pemblebrook Senior Living.

"Are you all right, sweetie?" Mrs. Dodgeson asked Erin as Mr. Dodgeson pulled out onto the road with Mrs. Wheeler in the front seat.

Erin hugged her mom, seeing how worried she was. "I'm okay, Mom."

And she really was. It wasn't a lie this time.

"Becca is too. We're okay."

"I don't like the idea of you letting a stranger in, but I think you did the right thing. She was just a confused old woman." Mrs. Dodgeson shook her head in disbelief. "I just have to wonder what on earth she had been thinking."

"She had a promise to keep," was all Erin said.

Epilogue

For the first time in over seventy years, Pemblebrook was without a ghost.

The nights following Patty's departure, Erin slept in Becca's room. She would lay awake in the middle of the night, listening for sounds of any ghost, but the house remained quiet. Serene.

Eventually she returned to her own room, but it wasn't because she couldn't stand sleeping in her sister's room anymore. It was merely because Erin knew that Becca was safe. That they both were.

Still, the experience had really shaken Erin. She understood how close she'd been to losing Becca, and it made her realize just how much she really loved her little sister and how her stubbornness to open up to her parents had been part of the problem.

So when Erin called Pemblebrook Senior Living about two weeks later to check on Mrs. Wheeler and was told she had passed away peacefully in her sleep, the first thing Erin did was talk to her mother. Mrs. Dodgeson was patient and understanding as Erin talked about Paula Wheeler and about how her death made Erin feel.

She told her mother that Paula's passing had made her feel confused, frustrated, and scared. But then, also relieved, knowing that Paula Wheeler had died in a way that seemed the most peaceful. That day, her mother and her talked, *really* talked. And though Mrs. Dodgeson didn't have all the answers, it made Erin feel better to just talk about it.

Just a couple months ago, Erin had longed to move to a big house in the country to get some distance from her family. Strangely, it had brought them closer than ever before. And Erin was all right with that.

The following Saturday after Paula Wheeler's death, Erin and her family decided to take another trip to Pemblebrook Park, where they would meet the Hollands for an end-of-the-summer picnic.

As Erin was taking things to the car, she heard the faint

sound of laughter. She stopped in the middle of the lawn and turned back to the large oak tree, knowing exactly where it was coming from. Under the heavy branches laden with green leaves, Erin could make out the treehouse and two profiles inside its window. Their gold hair glinted in the sunlight as their laughter carried on the summer breeze.

Acknowledgments

The first chapter of this book was written where all ghost stories should be told—in front of a campfire. So thanks for that truly inspiring writers' retreat in the foothills of Tennessee, RuthAnne. I can't wait to go back.

Thank you to my fantasic agent, Masha Gunic, and the team over at Azantian Literary Agency. My gratitude for your efforts to make this book a reality is beyond words.

A tremendous thank-you to Orlando Dos Reis, my amazing editor, who always finds the best ways to enhance my stories and up the spookiness level. And the rest of the team at Scholastic, Stephanie Yang, Mary Kate Garmire, Stephanie Cohen, Susan Hom, Marinda Valenti, Maddy Newquist, and Sarah Josprite—I'm so privileged to be working with you all.

About the Author

Lindsey Duga is a middle-grade and young adult writer with a passion for fantasy, science fiction, paranormal, and basically any genre that takes you away from the real world. She holds a bachelor's degree in mass communication from Louisiana State University and lives in Baton Rouge, Louisiana.